THE AGENCY
Volume Four

Burning Intensity

Icy Control

ELIZABETH
LAPTHORNE

The Agency Volume Four
ISBN # 978-1-78430-125-5
©Copyright Elizabeth Lapthorne 2014
Cover Art by Posh Gosh ©Copyright 2014
Interior text design by Claire Siemaszkiewicz
Totally Bound Publishing

Published in 2014 by Totally Bound Publishing, Newland House, The Point, Weaver Road, Lincoln, LN6 3QN, United Kingdom.

BURNING INTENSITY

Dedication

As always, with love and thanks to Lily, Billi and the ever-faithful Sue. Thanks for helping me so much, ladies, this would not be as wonderful without you. ☺

Chapter One

"This is the only chance you'll be given to avoid rotting in jail for the rest of your life," Eleanor Williams said as she walked into the cramped interview room. Her Agency partner Robert Stevens came in a few paces behind her.

The room was typical of any one of its kind around the world. Three bare, slate gray concrete walls kept the light from the florescent bulb quite dim. The fourth wall held the traditional one-way mirror. Any fool knew exactly what that mirror signified—that victims, family or management watched the discussion without wanting to be seen.

The thermostat controls remained perpetually a few degrees cooler than was considered comfortable. It was a purposeful, psychological prod to keep those being questioned off kilter. As part of her questioning technique, El frequently found it useful to be able to offer to turn the temperature higher when she wanted to appear courteous—the traditional 'good cop' routine.

Thaddeus Brown, however, seemed almost at home in the cool, depressing box. The solidly built, blond man lifted his gaze to meet hers as she faced him across the thin aluminum table. El knew her petite, short frame rarely intimidated anyone, let alone well-muscled, hardened thugs like Thaddeus.

Words could be quite powerful. El had long ago learned to wield them as sharply as any sword. She also knew her well-deserved self-confidence came across strongly in her body language. When needed, she could back up her physical self-assurance with actions. She worked and trained hard to keep in top shape and knew enough about a body's momentum to more than adequately make up for the difference between criminals who could be twice her size.

El didn't need to see behind her as the door thudded softly closed. She and Rob had worked together for years, been friends and partners for more than half her career. Trust bound them together more tightly than many lovers or siblings. Rob would almost certainly be leaning against the door, or wall, relaxed and appearing supportive and confident in her interrogation skills. At six foot four, he towered over practically everyone, but his height was always highlighted when he stood near her.

Powerfully built, Rob could have had almost any physical job he desired, from professional rugby player to a sleazy pub bouncer. Dark hair showed the first, faintest traces of gray, and his warm brown eyes could be frighteningly hard when Rob wished it so.

Sometimes he affected a bored look during their interviews — El knew that was a favored deception of his. Rob never lost focus, always tracking everything and retaining it for analysis later if needed. His control was icy and complete. She was a perfect counterpoint for him, her long, straight red hair being blamed for her passionate nature and usually fiery impatience.

They both knew with certainty that she could be patient and calm when needed, cool under fire. But she enjoyed getting information from reluctant people — the play of words, the dance and parry of matching wits. Rob plotted and planned — she reacted on the fly. As working partners, they were suited perfectly, their skills complementing and completing one another.

She loved him like a brother, trusted him unlike anyone else. Most of the time they were totally in synch, working as a pair and putting the worst of the bad guys away. While she loved Rob, it would never be a sexual thing — for either of them. El felt proud to defend her country, to do the work they did. It gave her a buzz she couldn't find any other way.

She rested her palms down on the table, then leaned in close, until her face was right up in Thaddeus' personal space. He met her gaze steadily, clearly unafraid of her or the power she wielded in this room.

"Why don't you start at the top," El cajoled. "Tell me everything."

El kept her gaze steady on Thaddeus. He watched her with an unblinking stare. El could see the reflection of her pale face in his orbs. They were now close enough that she could feel the faint puff of his breath as he exhaled.

She remained silent, letting the weight of the situation press down on him. After a full minute of mental fighting, Thaddeus scraped his chair back and put distance between them. Metal clinked — the cuff's chain knocked against the arm of the chair Thaddeus sat in.

His putting space between them was a small win, one that pumped adrenaline and more confidence through El.

Thaddeus ran a hand through his scruffy, sandy-colored hair. She could see in his eyes that something wasn't right. Over the years, she'd interviewed, interrogated and taken down countless criminals, many of them murderers with no conscience whatsoever. That hard, blank emptiness was something one couldn't overlook. After so much exposure to such people it didn't make her shiver anymore, or even blink.

El didn't move as Thaddeus ran his gaze slowly down her petite frame. She could feel the weight and heat in that glance, knew he was weighing her worth, judging her as a woman and an agent. El remained cool and calm. She'd been checked out by far creepier men than this. Her skin was thick and her tolerance for slime was high.

Any indication or acknowledgment would give him a sense of power and satisfaction. She watched him steadily, ignoring his lazy enjoyment and giving no outward response to him at all. But the more she surveyed him, the more she realized he wasn't the ordinary, garden-variety psychopathic killer she was used to. A vibe resonated from him, slowly filling the room.

"I'm sure it's not news to you, Mr Brown, that you're in a world of trouble," El began as she stood upright and placed her hands on her hips. Her tone was almost conversational, not hard or interrogating as yet. "We have substantial evidence to prosecute you. I've been informed the case we have on you is strong enough on its own merit. We don't need to lump you in with your co-conspirators. Let's see…"

Wanting to draw out the tension, El slowly lifted her head and caught Robert's gaze. She held a hand out, tilting her chin to indicate the files he held. Rob pushed his large frame away from the door and walked two paces into the room.

"Now, Brown, Brown," he played along as he flicked through the manila folders. "Ah, here we are. Thaddeus Brown."

Rob selected a folder and held it out to her. The corner of her mouth twitched in a tiny smile she knew her partner would catch, and took the paper from him. Opening the folder she then took her time to draw out every action. Feeling the tension crackling in the air, El held the folder in one hand and thumbed through the papers with her other. She pretended to read the printouts, rustling the file to keep Thaddeus' attention on the knowledge she had and he didn't. Instead of reading the file she already knew well, she scanned Thaddeus for reactions through her peripheral vision.

"Right." El flicked her ponytail over her shoulder and rapped the word out promptly, wanting to ratchet up the pace of the conversation once again. Moving from fast to slow like this, hopefully, would keep Thaddeus off balance and result in something new cracking open. "So far, the charges we're laying against you are really stacking up. We have multiple counts of illegal possession of restricted weapons—explosives, ammunition, numerous weapons themselves. Then we have smuggling, receiving and exporting of stolen and illegal items—that's two charges there—carrying concealed weapons, intent to cause bodily harm, premeditation of an assault against public property and destruction of property in general."

El felt proud of the smooth flow to her tone. She didn't hesitate over the complicated compilation of words. Indeed, the ease with which she listed his offenses washed through the room, frequently more powerful in these situations than fake bluster or arrogant posturing.

"And then we have my personal favorite and the current slam-dunk of our court system—domestic terrorism. That stunt you and your mates pulled at the National Gallery, it clearly falls under the new laws that have passed through. I'm sure you're aware of the changes to our Terrorism Act, and the harshness of those penalties. Times have changed, haven't they?"

El felt a small frisson of satisfaction as this, her final point, seemed to hit home. His eyes widened. There was no other indication that she'd managed to rock him and El was glad she'd caught the small giveaway. She didn't expect someone as hardened and unstable as Thaddeus to weep or bury his head in his hands, so this physical sign was akin to a scream of fright from him.

"Oh yeah," she purred as she closed the folder, dropped it onto the table and pressed her palms against the cool surface once again. Leaning close, she grinned. "This isn't your first time around this particular block, we all know that. The weapons, ammunition, even the devastation of property, those are all old hat to you, Brown. You can do the time on your head with one hand tied behind your back. We've no blushing virgins here. But terrorism? Ooh, that's a different level altogether."

Thaddeus narrowed his eyes to slits and he crossed one leg over the other in a defensive movement. She couldn't tell yet if he was starting to crack, or if these were small, unconscious tells. El didn't pause for breath, pressing the small advantage she held.

"Do you really think Kent and Luke aren't going to roll? I bet they're dancing to my colleague's tune already, handing out any information we wish and laying the bulk of the blame on you. I know you understand cooperation is key here, and the first person to help gets the plum deal. Your mates are the strategists, I can see that. You're just the weapons man, the boomer expert who keeps the artillery flush. Do you really think they aren't going to work their best to get their collective arse out of the fire?"

Experience coupled with her gut-deep instinct warned her that this man was highly dangerous, far more so than their usual suspects. The manner in which he skittered his glance around the room, coming back time after time to rest on her face, solidified the feeling that something wasn't right with him. If she hadn't been watching him so closely, she'd never have noticed how his breathing increased very slightly. That, coupled with his jerky gaze, made her wonder if he was a powder keg waiting to explode.

She finally found that label for Thaddeus she'd been searching for. The man was flat out crazy.

If he was, she knew he would go berserk and be an even greater threat to them all. Having long ago learned to never let her true emotions show while in interviews, El kept her expression even, not hinting for a moment that she had begun to get a picture of the depths and complexities in this man.

Despite the clear instability he possessed, there was certainly still intelligence flickering in Thaddeus. El knew he understood the airtight case they had against him and his co-conspirators. Yet he continued to remain silent as she gave a brief sketch outlining the strengths of the case they held.

Thaddeus sat up, but his muscles and posture remained relaxed.

Maybe he truly was crazy.

El stood again, reaching out swiftly with one hand to scoop up the file.

"They were right," El spoke, directing her words for the first time to Rob as she stepped away from the table. "He's not all there. We're wasting our time here."

"You have not, as yet, asked me a question," Thaddeus said in a calm, soft tone.

El paused, cocked her head to the side, then gave a single, curt nod. She gave him that point.

"My apologies," she replied formally, her tone as cool and low as his. "I'll make this extremely simple. Tell me where the Cezanne is, and I'll do what I can to stop you from being fried. There's no way out of this—you're all cooked—but there are harder ways to serve a multiple life sentence, and less hard ways. First one to point us correctly at the painting gets the less degrading, simpler route straight to hell."

Thaddeus frowned, the first seemingly normal, genuine response he'd given so far. "I don't know what trap you think you're setting out, but don't fuck with me or I'll happily go back to my comfortable cell and give you nothing. What do you really want?"

Now it was El's turn to struggle to restrain the surprise from crossing her face. Thaddeus' words were blunt and clear, his eyes cool and assessing, but free from guile. He honestly thought she was playing him.

"The whole point of your little spree was to compromise the security, create a cluster-fuck of confusion and upset security routines. This was to ultimately steal a little known Cezanne," El said slowly, clearly explaining the obvious to him. "Kent and Luke were the instigators, but you and the rest of your team successfully stole the painting. Despite the evident length of planning and detailed work the group of you did, during the few hours after your mission you were all scooped up and arrested. Are you denying you're a part of that team?"

"Lady, I'd happily lay siege all over again to the Gallery. Blowing those pillars up, getting to finally use my baby — the rocket launcher — fucking with the guards and compromising their precious system, not once but twice in less than twenty-four hours has been a highlight of my career. I'm not denying anything."

"So you're not interested in having a say on where you get to spend the rest of your life rotting away." El shrugged as she turned to face the door.

Thaddeus sighed. She tilted her head to look at him, but didn't move back to the table. El waited, patiently. Their gazes met. El showed nothing but self-confidence. Deep inside, she burned with a fire, knowing she was determined. She'd come out on top, regardless of how she made it there.

The air in the small room seemed to crackle with tension once again. Thaddeus was the first to glance away.

He sighed. "Kent and Luke didn't have the picture when you picked them up?"

"I wouldn't be here enjoying your company and asking you useless questions if they did," she pointed out reasonably.

Thaddeus shrugged. "I never laid a hand on the picture. How can I know where it ended up?"

"Why don't you make a guess and hope it pans out? Where do you think they might have kept it?"

Thaddeus frowned further, creases showing on his brow.

El remained still, frozen as she gazed steadily, taking in every inch of the criminal's posture and body language. He seemed to genuinely consider her question. When he licked his lips and lifted his eyes to her, she could see he'd decided to make an effort.

"Ask me something I can speak about," he said in a slow, clear tone. "Like those piece of shit weapons you're wearing—I can go on for hours offering solutions for better holsters, equipment or ammo. Talking about a painting I never personally laid eyes on isn't doable. What's so special about this picture, anyway? Kent never did tell me what the fuss was all about and why there was so much interest in it."

She wouldn't trust a word out of his mouth until she'd verified it, but at least this was something she could act on. Silence usually wasn't.

"Fuss? What kind of fuss happened over the piece?" El asked.

Thaddeus licked his lips again, a glint of something she couldn't label in his eyes.

"Thirsty work, talking," Thaddeus said with a smirk. "Any chance I can get some tea?"

El weighed the situation for a moment, then lifted her gaze to catch Rob's eyes. She nodded. He pushed away from the door again, opened it and stuck his head into the corridor. She heard the soft murmur of his voice, most of the words indistinguishable but 'tea' and 'plastic cup' letting her know her partner had the situation under control.

Robert finished, pulled himself back into the room and closed the door once again. He caught her gaze, nodded, and she threw a quick smile at him, thanking him silently. Knowing this could take a while, El pulled out the chair near her, opposite Thaddeus, and sat.

"So what kind of fuss brewed up over this painting and who else was interested in the Cezanne, Thaddeus?"

Thaddeus crouched, half standing in a bent over position so he could drag the chair closer to the table. This was difficult owing to the restraints chaining him hand and foot, but in a slow process he managed. El's body had tightened, her senses sharply aware as she watched him carefully, making sure he didn't palm a weapon or position himself in a manner that could let him spring on her or take advantage.

Satisfied when he sat back down and met her gaze again, she nodded for him to continue.

"I don't know who Kent—and Luke, I suppose— were going to sell the Cezanne to," he stated up front, his tone daring her to question him about it. "I overheard a number of conversations and phone calls, though. There was plenty of interest, and at one stage about six weeks ago I had the feeling there might have been another crew out there, wanting to get a jump on us and take the glory for themselves. As far as I'm aware, the plan was to sell the piece via silent auction after they'd gotten what they needed from the picture itself."

El's mind quickly jumped on the few important facts. If there had been another crew after the painting, Chelsea and David—the undercover agents they'd had on the inside of *this* team—had not been aware of it. Additionally, it appeared that the painting itself, while incredibly valuable and one of a kind, was not the final goal. Thaddeus had said 'once they got what they needed from it', which indicated that the painting itself held secrets.

The entire situation continued to grow more complicated.

Appearing to mistake her silence for annoyance, Thaddeus spoke again after a short pause.

"I'd guess the silent auction was to get the best price, or, hell, for all I know it was to offer the possible other group out to steal it a chance to recoup their reputation."

A knock interrupted. Rob blocked the entrance with his body, but opened the door to take the single disposable cup from another agent then closed it once again. Without a word, Robert placed the drink in front of Thaddeus, within reach of his chained hands.

El waited for their prisoner to carefully get hold of the cup, lift it to his lips and take a drink. It wasn't steaming, so El guessed it was the lukewarm tea available at one of the refreshment stations around the office. When Thaddeus had returned the tea, she started again, asking the same questions from a variety of angles— When had these calls taken place? Were they at specific times? International? From known associates or through third party contacts?

With patience she wrung Thaddeus dry. She leaned back only when she was confident he didn't have anything further to add. They had come up with a depressingly slim amount of new information, but she felt Thaddeus could add no more to their knowledge. Rolling her head back, El glanced at Rob, silently offering him a chance to jump in. If she'd missed something, forgotten to cover a point adequately, or if Rob had an idea on how they could gather more information, she wanted to give him the chance to get his bit in.

Rob's dark gaze met hers. He seemed to consider his thoughts for a few seconds, then gave a tiny shake of his chin, indicating that he couldn't think of anything to add.

El let the seconds draw out for a minute. Thaddeus didn't say a word, seeming happy to sit there until hell froze over. She was done, and Rob didn't want to add anything further. She stood.

"Either I or another Agent will let you know if this comes to fruition. Thank you for your assistance, Mr Brown."

She hadn't taken a step when Rob straightened and opened the door.

"Berecroft, Umbers, you can escort Brown back to solitary holding down on the third floor," Rob said in a clear voice to the agents out in the corridor.

El came to stand a pace behind Rob, feeling simultaneously pleased with their efforts and frustrated by the lack of closure.

She held her tongue as they both left the interview room. Without a word needing to be said between them, they headed down the corridor to where the lifts and fire exit stairs were situated. They climbed up three flights and left the stairwell, Rob courteously holding the door open for her.

"Thanks," she murmured distractedly as her mind flew over every word and nuance of the interview. El never took Rob's chivalry for granted, he was a gentleman to the core, but she wanted to go over everything again while it was fresh, be absolutely certain she hadn't missed anything.

On their regular floor, El slowed her pace as she thought hard. She walked more from habit than intention to the small area where their desks sat facing one another, carving out a small square of space where they worked, paced, brainstormed and discussed their cases.

'Office' was too generous a term for their space, though no other desks or cubicles were set up in the near vicinity. For an open plan area, they had as much privacy as was possible.

"It couldn't possibly have been simple, could it?" El groaned as she sat in her squishy chair, her body relaxing for the first time in the long day. Both she and Rob had been called in at around three that morning, once the Dublin agents who had been working undercover had realized the Cezanne they'd been trying to protect had not been with Kent or Luke—the smugglers whose ring they were breaking down.

"Thaddeus was our main hope for information." Rob shrugged. "Neither Kent nor Luke was interested in making a deal, that much was obvious from the start. You got a few nuggets from Thaddeus, enough for us to go on, that was brilliant work. Besides, we're the clean-up investigators, when are we ever called in for a simple, straightforward job?"

El rubbed tiredly at her eyes as Rob seated himself behind his desk, facing her.

"Have Chelsea and David headed back to Ireland?" she asked, hoping for a moment's diversion before they got back to the task at hand.

Rob studied her for a minute before he nodded.

"They're heading off on leave. After eighteen months deep cover and both of them getting pretty banged up at the end there, I'd say it's the least the Agency can offer. Chelsea seemed pissed off they didn't—couldn't—recover the Cezanne, but I think her attention is far more focused on David and the...uh...deepening of their relationship."

El smiled at Rob. While not strictly forbidden, it was heavily frowned upon to become intimate with your partner. Unless El was *way* off the mark, she felt certain that both Chelsea and David were deeply in love, and far more than casually intimate. Rob grinned, appearing to share her pleasure that they'd found happiness together.

Neither of them needed to speak of it. Spying was their bread and butter, a day-to-day occurrence. A low level of paranoia was imperative to both of their survival, so being circumspect about the stuff that really mattered was an ingrained habit. They were both pleased for Chelsea and David's happiness. Nothing needed to be said.

"At least we're not called in because of their injuries," Rob said, leading them back on topic.

"It makes a nice change," El agreed. "And I must admit to being curious as to what can be found within the Cezanne. Many people seem to have gone to great lengths to acquire it."

"Solving that puzzle isn't our current task," Rob chided her. "We're supposed to find the damn thing."

"First," El added as she raised an eyebrow.

Rob looked blankly at her.

"We're supposed to uncover the painting first. There's no reason we can't discover its secrets after that. We are supposed to be these brilliant problem solvers, after all. The fix-it partnership of our division."

"Management only wants us to find the artwork, wrap the project up into a neat little package and write an extensive report," Rob insisted.

El laughed. She could see very well that Rob, ever the analytical thinker, was searching for a way to toe the line but still have the answers she now knew they both sought.

For once, her colleague seemed almost as eager as she to delve into the intricacies of more than just answering the standard questions. It wasn't often that Rob's curiosity was piqued, but then he had a great appreciation for all manner of artwork. An impish delight flashed through her.

"You know who would be really helpful here?" She paused only a moment to be certain she had Robert's attention. With a grin, she continued before he could think of a response.

"Sally," she answered herself. "Think about it, mate. She's an artist, is already a known part of the art world. Sally has her delicate fingers in many pies and hears a lot of the stranger rumors and stories out there on all manner of artistic pieces and people. Maybe she knows something about this painting of Cezanne's."

El watched her colleague very closely as she spoke. At first his warm brown eyes lit with a thrill of anticipation. But then she could almost see him rein himself in, talk himself out of the strongly emotional response and into a more logical, analytical one. She had to resist thumping him over the head. The intensity of his desire for his oldest friend clearly burned through him, and yet he still resisted. El didn't really understand why.

Rob and Sally had known each other practically their whole lives. It was clear as crystal to her they adored one another. Yet for some reason—one she'd never felt confident enough to pry into—they remained just friends. This seemed and felt to El, instinctively, like the perfect opportunity to try to throw the two of them together.

"I really don't think—" Rob started as he straightened his spine, sitting up and looking uncomfortable.

El sighed with exasperation. She loved Rob, she truly did, but damn, he could over-think everything to death.

"She's been your friend forever. You trust her. You...care for her. If you can't turn to a friend like that when you need her help, who can you turn to? I bet Sally would love to hear from you. I've heard with my own ears you both promising to catch up more often, and then you get all distracted."

In truth she found Sally and Rob to be very similar at heart. They were both slightly odd, but gentle and with identical, kind souls. Robert certainly had harder edges, but inside he was soft as a teddy bear. Sally could be a little overly eccentric at times, and heaven knew she didn't over-think to the extent that Rob did. But, like him, she also had a giant heart and gentle way about her.

They were perfect for one another, if only she could open their eyes to it.

"If you must know," Rob said with only the faintest hint of exasperation directed her way, "I spoke to Sal only a few days ago. She's busy right now. She's finishing up a few more pieces for her new showing at another small gallery. She's thrilled, really excited about this opportunity, and I'm not going to ruin it for her by dragging her into the murky mayhem of my world."

El scooted her chair closer to her desk. She leaned her elbows on the smooth wood and tried to marshal her thoughts. She'd need a clear-cut argument, something that he couldn't out-think or out-argue. Before she could say a word or start to plan on the fly,

Rob raised his index finger to silence her and continued.

"We need to tap into a fence," he insisted.

El frowned, wondering what the hell a fence had to do with setting Sally and Robert up, but then she realized he was dragging them both—however unwillingly—back to the job.

"Certainly we need to speak to someone who knows the art world, but it needn't be an artist per se. We need someone connected, but also with their ear to the ground about all the shadier dealings. The underground markets, who will hear the whispers of 'Can you find me a—?' and 'Wouldn't it be lovely to purchase a—?' style conversations. A contact who knows all the current information about all the pieces going around."

El pressed her lips together and tried to think. She stubbornly clung to the desire to push Rob and Sally together.

"But Sally can—"

"You are the most tenacious woman alive, El," Rob replied with clear exasperation. He continued, his tone firmly insisting she fall into line. "We need someone trustworthy and reliable, but still shady. A person who can show an innocent face but still think deviously and bend the rules when we need. Someone whom both sides of the law can turn to and trust. A fence...or a thief."

"Sounds like an impossible person," El admitted, caught somewhere between wishful thinking and a hesitation she couldn't explain. "Now add on that they don't have the arrogance of a prince or the ego of a true diva and you might have found the perfect contact. Where do we find this paragon of a person? I can think of a few women who might fit a section or two of that enormous list, but—"

"Oh, no, I know just the man," Rob insisted, a smug smile on his face.

El tilted her head, still feeling a step behind her partner. She waved her hand in a 'come on' kind of motion, urging him to spill the secret name.

"Easy. We need James Waters."

El's jaw dropped and her cheeks flushed. Rob had to be paying her back for her pressing him about Sally earlier. She and James had a...complicated history between them. He was a thief and a scoundrel and, and... Well, it was complicated.

"You have got to be kidding me," she finally stammered.

Rob shook his head. His tone was completely serious, his dark gaze steady. "He's perfect."

"He's..." The words died on her tongue. El closed her eyes, drew in a deep breath and prayed for strength. She'd seen that spark in her partner's eyes before. Rob had earlier called her tenacious. She was a novice compared to him when it came to stubbornness. "I want to veto," she insisted.

"I didn't veto Sally," Rob replied, his tone deceptively mild. "As I explained, she's busy with her own work and can't help right now. That's not the same as a veto for no real reason."

El groaned again, knowing already that she was going to lose. Rob had given a perfectly truthful, and logical, explanation as to why they couldn't ask Sally for assistance. El and Rob had a strict rule of only being able to veto an idea or suggestion if the other already had—to keep things balanced between them. The only other way she could veto was if her argument convinced Rob to let it go. Her heart pounding, cheeks flushed and her mind racing, El wasn't at her cool, logical best. That knowledge didn't deter her.

"But this is James."

"Exactly. He's the best suited to the task."

"But this is James."

"That's not a solid enough argument to win a veto from me. Are you even trying?"

El took another breath and tried to think of a smart, snappy answer. Her mind remained frozen, blank.

"But this is James." She slumped her shoulders, knowing she'd lost.

Chapter Two

"Surely someone else owes us a favor or three," El spoke for the first time since they'd left the office.

For the most part the silence between them had been comfortable. Both she and Rob were well used to their own thoughts, the need for a constant flow of nervous or uneasy chatter long gone. Rob had found a park for their car a few short streets away from James' flat. They walked the rest of the distance together, their paces evenly matched and now so natural it was routine for them.

"I notice you didn't call ahead," El pressed Rob. "James isn't expecting us yet. Surely we can call in a few markers? Or even cold canvass some of the experts at the National Gallery. I bet—"

"I'm certain it hasn't slipped your mind that the National Gallery is only a step up from smoldering rubble right now," Rob replied.

"The building still stands," she insisted stubbornly.

"Barely. Are you really going to press this point?" Rob halted and they faced each other.

El had to tilt her head up, but she pressed her hands to her hips, her head tossed back, more than willing to stand behind her point…if only she could admit the full depth of it.

Evidently seeing her determination, Rob sighed. His shoulders eased down and the moment of possibly genuinely arguing passed.

"No one is as good as Jimmy," Rob said. "You know it and I know it. I know you're not seeing one another right now—but we all got together, what? Six months ago? The two of you were very…cozy together. If he hurt you, or if something truly bad had occurred you'd have told me. I know that. But if you really, truly don't wish this we can try another way. But we both know he's our best chance."

El pressed her lips together, torn and not certain what to say to that. There was so much truth to Rob's words, but she couldn't just capitulate.

"You know how good he is," Rob insisted.

"He's a risk taker," she replied.

"He takes calculated risks, that's a very different thing," Rob said.

"Okay then, he's dangerous."

Her words baffled Rob, she could tell by the blank, surprised look on his face.

"Really? What? How do you mean?"

Rob's gaze sharpened on her and for a moment she worried he could see clear through to her soul. They knew each other so well, but still there were pockets neither ever let the other into—private sections they both respected and steered clear of.

"I've never seen that from him," Rob said gently, clearly caught between caution and curiosity. "Or not genuine dangerousness. He's always struck me as a fellow who goes to great lengths to protect himself—

and us, if you recall. Do enlighten me on how, exactly, you find him dangerous, El."

El felt for a moment as if a careful trap had surrounded her. Her words had been instinctive, she hadn't meant to consciously speak them. Of course she'd meant that James was dangerous to her, her heart, her sanity. Rob seemed to have guessed this now, and El wasn't sure how to get herself extracted from it. She knew she could come to rely on James Waters far, far too much. He could be everything to her, hold her body and soul. But damned if she'd admit that, not to herself and not to Rob, either.

"Oh, fine, he's not dangerous in the least," she grumbled.

Rob tilted his mouth into a small, knowing grin. El continued down the road to James' flat. After a few paces, she heard the clomp of Rob's boots following her, catching up in a couple of strides.

For a minute she waited, her breath held. Part of her desperately hoped Rob wouldn't question her further. Her friend and partner all too often saw far too much, the intelligent, analytical side of his brain putting random pieces of the puzzle together with stunning clarity.

Thankfully, he appeared focused on his own musings. El heaved a sigh of relief. That conversation would come back, she knew. But later was always preferable to sooner, to her mind. She looked up as they came to the front gate of James' flat. Rob had been right—as usual—it had been nigh on six months since she'd been here. No way would she have guessed she'd be back so soon, nor under such strange circumstances, but life was often a bitch like that.

Taking in a careful breath, El led the way up the short path and rapped on the door. It was still morning, well before lunch, but the stillness emanating from inside the flat had hope sparking in El's chest. Maybe James had gone out somewhere, or, better yet, moved.

She tilted her face up, a smile on her lips as she was about to speak to Rob, when she heard movement come from inside.

So much for that hope, she sighed.

Turning back to face the door, not bothering to say anything since Rob almost certainly knew the gist of what she'd been about to say, El tried to settle her pounding heart.

"Coming," James' voice sounded muffled from behind the door.

She was about to reply that there was no rush—even a few seconds gave her more time to get her wayward emotions under control—El's attention was caught by Rob. His large body flexed as he tilted to the side, peered farther down the road.

"Oh look," he commented placidly, his tone idle, "that's interesting. I'm just going to go over here. No, no, you stay here, El. Talk to James."

With a far too innocent, vague expression on his face, Rob turned and walked back to the footpath and ambled down the road. His hands were thrust into the pockets of his slacks, his pace an easy, relaxed stroll. Not even in her wildest dreams could El have convinced herself there was something wrong, or a need for her to race into action.

Rob, she knew without a doubt, hadn't found anything 'interesting'—or not unless you counted her partner wanting to give her privacy to talk with James. Rob was giving them space. El didn't know whether she wanted to shoot her partner in the kneecap, or thank him for his perception and delicacy.

The loud click of the door being unbolted captured her attention. El still hadn't fully prepared herself, but it was too late now. James stood before her.

He had the flushed, rumpled appearance of the recently roused. If his hair had been longer, it would have been tousled, but she noticed that he'd kept it short. Warm blue eyes were still languid and sleepy, his jaw and chin stubbled with dark blond hair. El's breath caught as her gaze lowered. James' broad, well-muscled chest was naked, his skin smooth, and she knew it would be warm to her touch.

Well-worn tracksuit pants had slid low on his hips. Only the fact that they were extremely baggy hid what she suspected would be a morning erection. The thin trail of hair ran in an enticing, delicious line from his navel, down the smooth line of his flat belly, daring her to lick along it and find the treasure at its base. She'd done exactly that in the past, and lust burned through her, tempting her to repeat the experience.

A surprised sound, part grunt, part gasp, came from James.

El's gaze snapped back up and their eyes met. James looked shocked, almost as if he'd woken from a dream.

"Well, shit," he cursed. He stepped back and slammed the door shut in her face.

El blinked, caught somewhere between annoyance and laughter.

Apparently she wasn't the only one off balance. Seeing James again, the intoxication of having his mostly naked body so close and yet still utterly out of reach, had jumbled her every sense. The door was again wrenched open and James stood before her once more, blinking as he wiped the sleep from his eyes.

She sadly noticed that he'd tugged his pants up and slipped on a large, old T-shirt. El privately admitted she'd hoped to see more of his body. The fact that her desire could have a bent for the masochistic was shocking. She couldn't think of a more bizarre form of self-inflicted torture, lusting after what was out of her reach.

James crossed his arms and peered down the street. Owing to Rob's height, he was still visible. Rob turned, as if he could feel their gaze on him. El chuckled as Rob caught her glance and raised his hand. He sketched them a cheery wave.

"He's giving us space?" James asked.

El nodded. "Appears to be."

El found herself shifting from foot to foot, then forced herself to stop. The silence between them was charged, not just with latent, powerful sexual chemistry — for that had always lain between them — but also with the weight of things unsaid, and words that had been exchanged, promises made the last time they'd been together.

It was completely uncharacteristic for her to shy away from speech, from doing what was right, necessary. Yet pain lurked beneath the surface between them. Hurt, rejection and a whole host of other complicated emotions swirled and built up.

El decided the longer she put this off, the harder and more devastating it could be. In truth, she'd already put it off months longer than she should have.

Never in the past had she taken the coward's route, the easy way out. The only result of those actions had been to postpone the pain and make it worse. She needed to make this right. Things mightn't be the same between them, but she would not use James. She couldn't bear to have him question her intentions, to lay that sin at her door with the others.

El met his gaze, relishing the warmth in those blue eyes, despite the pain and confusion also clear in his face.

"I'm actually here to ask for help. Something's come up and... But now I'm here... Well..." she struggled.

James waited patiently, his features not betraying much. He seemed willing to hear her out, but not inclined to help her or to make this easier than necessary.

Since she was the one in the wrong here, she couldn't fault him for that.

El straightened her shoulders, took a deep breath and steadied herself. She held his gaze, opening herself unflinchingly to him.

"I've been wrong, and I owe you an apology for that. Can I come in, please? So we can talk?"

"About work?"

"That too, but first I can try and explain."

"I've always listened to you," James said slowly, seeming to measure his words before he spoke them. "And since you're being honest, I can be so too. I'm angry, and upset, but I'm also interested in why you never called. I've not known you to go back on your word, but... Okay, come on in. Let's do this inside."

James stepped back and held the door open for her.

She shouldn't have been surprised, but his flat had changed very little in the last few months. A large, open plan space made the tiny flat appear roomier than many others of its kind. A small kitchenette took up one corner, with a large window that let the sun shine in and was home to a number of small pots of various herbs. Cleaned dishes had dried in their rack overnight and, while not spotless, the main living area was clean.

James silently led her over to the long couch, pushing the low coffee table far against the wall to give them both more leg space. Framed prints hung on the walls and gave color to the atmosphere.

"You haven't changed a lot in here," El said as she removed her jacket, folded it and placed it out of the way on the table.

James sat, a small smile on his face. "I haven't put the crown jewels on display yet, no."

El chuckled, reminded of how easily they had teased each other despite their differences. "You've never been the flamboyant kind, not privately at least."

"I'm devastated," James mocked her, a palm pressed dramatically to his chest. "Would it be easier if I act more the part of the arrogant, playboy thief for you? I can offer you a tour of my etchings? Invite you into the back room where I have all manner of priceless art, jewels and sculptures stashed away? Since we're such good friends I won't even ask for a warrant. You can arrest me. We've always had a penchant for playing cops and robbers."

This time El did laugh. The truth in his words both stung and comforted in their familiarity.

"You've not complained about my interrogation techniques before," she replied lightly as she sat, her legs angled to the side so they faced each other. James' gaze sharpened and the teasing, relaxed manner stiffened.

Once again unspoken, leaden sentences remained heavy in the air. James' mouth thinned as he pressed his lips together. "No, I never complained. But then, it was your lack of words that hurt me. You never called."

El fluttered her eyes closed. She could hear the weight in what he said, the depth of feeling clear behind each syllable.

Opening her eyes, El frowned. "I didn't mean to cause you pain. I know that doesn't help, but it's the truth. All of this, the feeling of betrayal, it was the last thing I wanted."

"You promised to call and I believed you. When you said it was complicated, that it would take time to sort out, that didn't bother me. I understand a lot of what you do has a forest of non-disclosure statements attached to it. That's part of the package that comes with you and something I can accept. Do you know how stupid I felt, rushing home every night to check my messages, hoping and being deflated day after day? I always thought people who stuck close to the phone, moping because a lover didn't call them, were pathetic. I have a healthy amount of sympathy for them now."

James looked up and their gazes met. El didn't turn away or flinch as he finished, His pain was clear to see, both in his features and within his speech. She waited a moment when he was done, assimilating everything he'd showed her, but also probing her own heart. She promised herself she wouldn't hurt him again, not if she could possibly help it.

If that meant she needed to walk away, regardless of the price she'd pay for that action, she would. James already knew the bare basics of her work. He was aware that she was employed by an agency of the government to investigate people and situations the police and other, more public faces couldn't sully themselves with. James' connections with many gray area artists, business people and the fringe elements of higher society had drawn them together on a previous case.

The fact that she'd discovered he had a wide range of skills as a thief, that he had knowledge of security systems and how to get around them, had only deepened her interest in him. After almost a month of dancing around each other — physically and verbally — they'd fallen into bed together, and El had found her heart on the brink of being stolen by his fast, slick, delicate and talented hands. James thrilled and scared her on many levels. Their passion and lust burned with an intensity she'd never experienced before. Being with him, the intimacy of their growing relationship was akin to being in a free fall.

Powerful, terrifying and exhilarating all at the same time.

James was addictive, but the complexities woven between them made her feel like she had lost her mind to open herself to him.

But he was a trustworthy man. El never doubted that for a moment.

James was a gentleman to his core. When he gave his word, he stuck to it no matter what the cost.

She needed to be honest with him — or as open as she could be.

El shifted closer to him on the couch, so their knees were only a few inches apart. Folding her hands in her lap, she then linked her fingers, her gaze down but unfocused. She collected her thoughts, took a deep breath and lifted her face. Meeting his gaze, opening herself as much as possible, she groped for the words to explain without breaking her promise to the Agency and telling him too much.

"You know I was messaged and then called in that afternoon. It was my day off, but I knew something big was going down. My team leader added in a code word to the text he sent. A single word can't come close to explaining the complexities of what was really happening, but it indicated there'd been an internal betrayal, a traitor. I'd heard murmurs already, but still I was shocked by the messy web we'd been dragged into."

El tightened her fingers together as she recalled the nightmare of paperwork, distrust amongst colleagues, and the level of paranoia for months that had skyrocketed almost out of control. Spies were naturally cautious creatures—they didn't live, otherwise—but knowing one of their own had been actively causing them harm, betraying them, had sent out waves of repercussion that still were not fully healed.

She genuinely believed that the worst had passed, but the actions of a few horrible people had left scars, both on the Agency, the managers and particularly the good men and women who worked there.

"Rob and I are often called in once a mission has gone to shit, we're used to that. But this was far above and beyond anything we usually come across. It also wasn't just us. There were teams of agents pulled together." El pressed her fingers between her eyes, massaged the bridge of her nose. She could almost feel the headache she'd had for weeks back then. "We were on shifts, sleeping for a few hours at a time on cots in the locker room... I could go on if you need, but you get the idea. At first I thought it would be a week, maybe two tops to get everything under control. But it was longer than that, and so much more complicated."

"I knew you were facing a crisis," James assured her.

El slumped her shoulders down. She could feel the warmth in his tone, sense the tenderness from the soft way he looked at her.

"I was prepared to wait, I told you that. You're worth every moment, Eleanor."

"It was almost two months before the reports were written," she continued. El cleared her throat, embarrassed at how husky her voice sounded. She blinked hard, swore it wasn't tears at his compassion but just an eyelash, maybe. "If I'd known how convoluted it would all be, how the days would blur and weeks would fly by, I'd have sent a message, texted you, done something to indicate it would be far worse than I'd ever have imagined. But by the time my brain cleared and I glanced around, it had been so long. When I thought of how you'd have been waiting, every day far slower and longer than it had been for me..."

El shook her head.

"I threw myself into the meetings—and trust me, you don't want me to start explaining what those were like. Endless. Painstaking. A nightmare in and of themselves. I kept telling myself you wouldn't have waited, or that you would have called me. Anything to sop the guilt and loneliness I felt with your absence."

"You told me not to call," James replied with a frown.

El reached out a hand, took his in hers.

"I know, I didn't mean I blamed you. Nor was this all some elaborate ploy for you to prove yourself to me, I promise. But I needed to rationalize my actions. It was so long, it felt like I was so late... Like I'd missed my chance. Besides, by then I was at the stage where the longer I put it off, the harder the mere thought of reconnecting with you became."

She swallowed, then licked her lips. El was nervous, but determined to be brutally honest and explain her actions as best she could.

"It was easier for me to focus on contingencies at work, on helping plug the leaks that we'd found from the traitor's deception. I wanted— No, I *needed* to help other agents who were in deep cover, give them any assistance they needed in solidifying their position. There was an endless amount of work to do, and hard as that was, it wasn't as emotional as picking up the phone and asking you to meet me for coffee."

"You were afraid I'd moved on?" James asked. He'd lifted an eyebrow at her.

El didn't know whether he was teasing her or couldn't believe her, but at least he didn't seem upset. She smiled at him, squeezed his hand gently.

"We hadn't made promises to one another. It's not like we were engaged or promised. But..." *Honesty,* she reminded herself, difficult as it was. She scrunched her face a little, forcing herself to bare her soul. James deserved it, was worth it. "I was afraid you'd reject me, lash out in anger. I honestly didn't mean to leave you hanging, to hurt you. But I couldn't have blamed you for being bitter or furious either. You had every right to demand answers or rail at me. I care about you. I feel vulnerable, exposed when you get that hot look in your eye. This passion between us, it was never casual to me. To have you angry or dismissive of me could tear strips from my heart. Again, it was easier to just keep pushing forward and work, work, work."

James shifted slightly. Whether on purpose or not, El couldn't help but be thrilled when he touched his knees against hers. He squeezed his fingers around hers. El's heart raced. This was the first positive indication she'd had from him. Her cheeks flushed warmly, her pale skin betraying the rise in her spirits and temperature.

"Is it over?" he asked, his tone husky.

El grimaced, shrugged a shoulder.

"We've contained the damage as much as possible. Waldron—" she caught herself, reminded that she needed to be careful of how close she pushed to the line of breaking her confidentiality agreement. She thought for a second, then continued. "My team leader, Waldron, put Rob and me back on other tasks about six weeks ago. The Agency is still trying to recover, not just emotionally but also from the mammoth proportion of the breach. We lost some agents, and I was friendly with a few of them. Everyone seems to know someone who was compromised. There are also quite a few gaps in intel that we've lost and can't account for. Stuff like that. The bulk of the clean-up is finished and the board's discussing countermeasures. For most of us, though, we're back to business. Battered and bruised, but back."

"I knew it was bad," James said in a soft tone. "And I know you've only scraped the surface for me. But even so, it sounds awful. I'm sorry."

"Don't be. I let myself get too caught up in it. When I finally came up for air, I let my fear, pride and doubt cloud my judgment."

"You weren't the only one too proud to reach out and try to communicate. It's not like I don't know your number by heart," he pointed out.

El grinned wryly. "It was I, as I recall, who promised to call."

"Did you want to?" James' warm blue gaze sparkled like a crystal as they searched each other's eyes. El felt lost in him, could sense that strange phenomenon of falling into him. This time, unlike the others, she trusted him implicitly—to catch her and hold her safe—and let herself go.

"Yes. I wanted to. Badly. But at the same time I couldn't bring myself to."

Time seemed suspended. El had never felt this with anyone else. The outside world, all the problems and issues faded back to white noise in the background. The Cezanne, her mission with Rob, all the pain and awkward emotions that had built up between her and James—it all melted away into nothing.

They turned simultaneously to face each other, their knees bumping. Heat seared through her body. She could feel the warmth of his skin, even through the thin material of his tracksuit pants.

"We're both proud, stubborn people, really, aren't we?" he mused.

El chuckled. "At least we're not as different as we first thought. A thief and a spy—you'd think we'd be oil and water."

"Doesn't matter what we are," James insisted, his voice thick with need. His eyes burned so hotly she felt amazed her skin didn't scorch. Heart hammering, her throat dry with desire, El tilted her head toward him, lifting her lips, needing to feel the hot press of his body upon hers.

"We were fools," he murmured.

El lifted her hand, threaded her fingers through the short strands of his hair. Cupping the back of his skull, she helped guide his lips to hers. She exerted almost no pressure—he'd seemed to have the same thought as she.

They joined their mouths together, and heat pulsed through her body. His lips were soft, even more so than she recalled in her dreams. El moaned as her nipples peaked, hungry for his touch. Shifting her thigh restlessly, she could feel moisture slicking across her pussy lips. El pushed her feet to the floor, keeping their mouths fused together as she bent over almost double. She turned, straddled James' thighs and sat in his lap. Heat radiated from his thick shaft.

Groaning, she tilted her hips, pressing her apex hungrily into his erection. They moved their hands over each other's body. Tingles of pleasure arced over her skin where he touched her. Focused on stripping him, she didn't even notice as he unbuttoned and removed her shirt.

"Do you know how much I've missed this? How much I've longed for you?" she murmured as she dropped his T-shirt to the floor. She sighed at the smooth, muscled expanse of his chest, finally bared once again to her ravenous gaze.

Dipping her head down, she began to lick a slow, hot trail along his skin. The deep rumble of need—part groan, part gasp—sounded like it had been torn from his soul. It only spurred more hunger through her blood. El tilted her head back, so she could continue to touch him, taste him and watch him simultaneously.

His eyes flared with heat, a fiery passion she knew could prove beyond addictive. Matching him pace for pace, she let all her hunger reflect back to him in her gaze, in every caress of her fingers.

Heat prickled along her skin and she knew her pale complexion would be flushed pink. James stroked her hair, then wrapped a few of the straight tendrils around his fingers, tugging her gently closer.

"I missed you too," he admitted. "Missed this. I craved you. Dreamt of you. I'm not ever letting you go again."

She smirked, not just pleased, but thrilled at the possessive tone to his voice. Opening her mouth, she was about to repeat his words back at him, but he clasped his hands over her arms and dragged her higher. She arched her back and he stole her breath away. James closed his lips ferociously around one lace-clad nipple.

He sucked on her and all thought, all reason fled. El let herself give up control. She let her head fall gracefully back, her ponytail swishing across her bare skin, further sensitizing her and heightening her arousal.

The world receded—only James and her desperate need for him existed.

Chapter Three

Part of James' brain couldn't wrap itself around the knowledge that El was here, in his lap, on his couch, with him again, at last. If he couldn't feel her weight on his thighs, smell that faint scent of jasmine from her perfume and hear those throaty, decadent sounds she made when aroused, he'd have been tempted to believe he was having another one of *those* dreams.

But she was here. With him. *Finally*.

It took a minute for him to follow his fingers to his brain's direction, to unsnap her bra and let it fall away. Her breasts were a perfect handful, pert and soft to the touch. He stroked the pad of each thumb over her nipples, arousing them to hard little peaks.

El's eyes were enormous, the pale blue irises just a thin ring around the large black pupils. Her delicate, pale skin was stained with the rush of blood beneath it—but he adored her like this, lost to all reason, burning up for him and because of his actions. Her deep red hair had been one of the first things he'd noticed about her, the silky tendrils that looked luscious spread out on his pillow.

Gently he pulled the elastic from her hair, sighing happily as the burgundy locks cascaded past her shoulders and down her back in a straight curtain. He'd always been a sucker for a redhead. El was different, though—special. He planned to prove that to her here and now. He couldn't make it to the bed, comfort and tradition be damned.

He knew that something serious had brought her to his door. Robert wouldn't have joined her had this been a personal call. James knew their time would run out all too soon, and he wanted to indulge in every second granted to him.

Cupping one perfect breast in the palm of his hand, he paused a moment to enjoy the full, heavy weight. He lifted the mound, then bent down and suckled on the nipple. El cried out, an inarticulate sound filled with need and pleasure. He could never forget that sound, or mistake it for anything else. Her breaths came in short, sharp pants, the sexual flush moving down her neck and starting to cover her chest. The cadence of her moans rose—and he knew she was close.

Feeling wicked, wanting to sate her, but also prove to her just how much they needed each other, he quickly opened her pants and loosened the waistband. Suckling harder on her breast, he drew on the nipple, knowing from her previous confessions that it sent pleasure shooting downward, through her belly right to her clit, igniting her pussy.

He mumbled against her skin, the vibration adding to the sensations he built within her. James watched her, drank in every move, every line of that beautiful face, the graceful sweep of her neck, the arch of her back. She mesmerized him, and for the first time since his youth, James felt the urge to sketch. He had only a little talent, but something about El resonated deeply within him and he wanted to capture that. Create it over and over.

El groaned as he slid his fingers inside her lacy knickers. Even with only a few of his brain cells working, his digits knew precisely what to do. Fingers fluted, he stroked into her warm flesh, parting her labia and sliding deeper. James left one finger behind to caress her clit, but then he probed the others farther, finding her opening wet, hot and sensitive enough that he could tell from her tone she was perched on the edge of climax.

"Come for me, beautiful," he said softly around her breast. "Come only for me, show me that glorious moment you achieve ecstasy."

El grasped his shoulder, her hand slipping for a moment as she appeared overwhelmed with pleasure. She found purchase and cracked her eyes open. Their gazes met and he held her, wanting them to share her first peak. With shuddering breaths, she rocked her hips forward, riding his hand. James hissed in pleasure, his cock straining against his pants, desperately craving his own release.

Forcing himself to not just lose control, pull himself free and plunge into her, he struggled and watched her like a man possessed. She thrust her pussy over him and he pumped his fingers harder, faster, deeper.

"James," she panted. Her words were thready, coherence clearly beyond her. "More. Please. Now. Fuck."

Lifting her breast higher, he then lightly grazed his teeth over the sensitive tip, blowing on the wet nipple before he poked his tongue out and laved at her. He worked his hand faster in her pants, and El was thrusting onto him at a strong pace, evidently on the brink.

Six months could be a lifetime, he had learned, but some things never changed. Watching El fall apart, drinking in every delightful, luscious moment as she came hard and strong was better than anything he'd ever known. Her body lifted, her breast falling from his mouth. Her head fell back, her lips parted and she lifted her eyes to the ceiling. With her back arched, she reached her free hand out, and James could feel the ripples of her pussy sucking down, milking his fingers as her orgasm washed over her.

It took a minute for the rest of El to catch up.

She screamed, loudly enough that he worried for a second that the neighbors would call the police.

"Fuck yes," James murmured, enchanted. "That's it, beautiful, come for me. Oh, you're gorgeous."

El clutched at him and after a minute she sank against him, her breasts pressed to his chest, her head resting on his shoulder. She panted and despite the aching fire of desperate need in his crotch, he felt deeply satisfied, smug in a masculine way that was not arrogance, merely fact.

He pressed a kiss to the tender place beneath her ear and felt the soft, warm glow of love in his heart. He'd rather cut his tongue out than speak of it, especially after the rollercoaster they'd both been on, but he knew in his soul there was no other woman alive for him. Only El. This time, he swore she wouldn't get away.

It had been six long, unbearable months since she'd felt James' touch. There'd been no one since him or for quite a while before him, either, but El never would have guessed that a bit of a suck on her breast and a few strokes of his fingers would have her coming harder than she could recall experiencing before.

Sure, the man had magic fingers — in a number of respects — but really, she couldn't believe it had only needed a bit of a lick and tickle.

"You didn't make it to the party," she murmured as she lifted her head from his shoulder. Swiping her hair from her eyes, she smiled at her lover.

"We're only beginning," he replied. His eyes shone and she could hear the happiness in his tone, that faintly smug, male satisfaction she often heard from him when he felt pleased with himself.

Grinning, she tilted her head and softly kissed him. They explored tenderly with their lips. Re-learning each other with a slow, easy pace. Opening her mouth she then flicked her tongue out, tangled it with his and enjoyed the stirring she felt in her body. The knot of tension she'd held in her belly had disintegrated upon her climax, but flames once again licked at her as the ever-present chemistry between them ignited her senses once again.

James stroked her inner walls with his fingers and her body jolted — the pleasure ratcheting up once again. El lifted her hips, one hand lowering to gently remove him from her pussy.

"Easy, tiger," she panted, her need already spiraling out of control again. "You've taken the edge off — six months is quite a celibacy stretch — but this time I want to come with you, not by myself."

She met his gaze, faintly chagrined that she'd admitted to him that she'd not been touched since the last time they'd seen one another. El was both pleased, and embarrassed, that it was out there now. James' eyes were soft — she got the feeling he was happy with her comment.

"I haven't wanted anyone else either. You didn't need to tell me, but thank you."

Grinning wickedly now, she used her thighs to push his legs apart. Reaching a foot carefully down to the floor, she got her balance, opened his legs and knelt between them. With a palm to each of his hips she scooted him forward so he sat on the edge of the couch. Mimicking his earlier motion, she dipped her hands beneath the elastic waistband of his pants and pushed the thin material down so his thick, long length sprang free.

Slick with juices, stiff as a board and flushed a dark color, James' erection was a welcome sight.

"Mmm," she murmured. She licked her lips, recalling vividly the numerous times she'd sucked him off with great enthusiasm. She loved to drink him down. It gave the added side-benefit of taking the edge off for him before he pounded into her, fucking her blind, deaf and absolutely dumb.

She was beyond eager for an encore. It had been forever.

Wrapping her fingers around his base, she spent a moment stroking the crinkly hairs protecting him.

"When you opened the door and I saw your little trail, I wanted to do this," she confessed, her voice incredibly thick and husky. Deciding they could talk later, she moved closer, tilted her head and licked from his navel, down his flat tummy, and followed the enticing path of faint, short hairs.

James shuddered and she recalled in a blinding flash that he was particularly sensitive on the skin beneath his belly.

El murmured, but the words all jumbled together, her brain frying as instinct took over. A hot flush of need washed over her as she was delighted by his words. Lightly, with infinite care and tenderness, she scraped her teeth over his skin. His body twitched and she knew the reaction was part ticklish, part sexual ecstasy. She repeated the caress, licking the spot for good measure.

This elicited a groan of approval. James canted his hips up, his cock rigid and hot with need. The hand that held him grew slick with his juices. El moved lower, but took her time to nibble and thoroughly enjoy every inch.

Finally her chin bumped against the wobbling head of his shaft. Opening her jaw, she flicked her tongue out, tasting his salty pre-cum.

"Oh, El, oh please, yeah," he moaned.

Seeming lost, his eyes closed and his face twisted with bliss, James reached out and cupped her jaw, drawing her farther down his shaft. Eager to oblige, she relaxed her throat and swallowed him down as far as she could.

Hot and thickly erect, he filled her mouth and throat. The sheer power in him had her wet once again. El bobbed her head, sucking hard on him and pumping his cock with her hand. She gently played with his balls, the furred sac tight and high, warm with his seed.

Breathing hard as her own arousal rose, El moved over him, working her jaw, caressing him faster with her hands as pleasure bloomed through her. Small sounds of passion fell from his lips and she stole glances at him as he lost himself to her ministrations.

All too soon she felt the faint tremor, the rumble in his body as his muscles contracted, readied themselves for his release.

"Oh yeah, I'm almost there, El," he warned her.

Craving to taste his essence, she pressed her tongue against his shaft, working hungrily, wanting to have everything. He shouted, a hoarse, strangled sound. His body seized up, muscles bunching as his hips thrust in hard, sharp bursts. He plunged his cock deeper down her throat, threatening to choke her.

El drew in a deep breath and relaxed. Hot gushes of seed pumped into her, filling her mouth with a musky, salty fluid. Swallowing, she took it all, repeating the gesture as he shot into her over and over again. The convulsive tightening of her mouth and throat as she swallowed massaged his stalk, urging him to continue until she'd wrung him dry.

James fell back against the couch, seeming replete. He panted, shuddering with deep breaths that proved to her how hard he'd come. El lapped at his shrinking cock, her hands still sticky but unwilling just yet to relinquish him. When she was certain that he'd finished, she lifted her head, tasting her lips and taking every last piece of him into her.

Bending toward him, she then pressed small, hot kisses against his flat belly. He groaned, though the sound had nothing to do with pain and everything to do with passion. She watched him as he squeezed his eyes shut, then cracked one open and glanced at her.

"You know what that does to me," he chided her teasingly.

She grinned, not needing to say a word. Instead she naughtily kissed him again, this time scraping her teeth around his belly button.

Pressed against him, she could feel the twitch of his muscles and the stirrings of interest in his cock. Her grin became a wide smile, lust filled her and her heart sped up. Her pussy ached for him, needing to feel his thick length penetrating her once again, pulsing within her and possessing her body and soul.

She craved him.

"Insatiable woman," he murmured, need and lust bright in his gaze. "Do you know how often I've dreamed of you? Of this? I'm going to fuck you harder than you believed possible. And then, once I've filled your pussy with everything I can, I plan to work around to that arse of yours. We never did get there last time, did we? I love that you've never had your anus reamed, El. It's one hell of an experience, or so I've been told. A bit of preparation, some stretching or maybe a toy or two and I bet I can have you screaming for mercy and pleading for more."

His words couldn't have had more of an effect upon her if he'd electrocuted her. Desire, need, raw craving flooded her. The mental image he portrayed, of his cock thrusting up her arse, possessing her in the most intimate way imaginable, had her hot and ready right now. Words failed her. She could only gape at him, the sensual fantasy he wove intoxicating her.

James seemed to read her very well and his grin deepened, the twinkle in his eye now wicked with a sensual, vengeful lust.

"Oh yeah, El. I might even restrain you, gag that luscious mouth of yours, though maybe I'd prefer to hear your cries. Do you have any idea how perfect you look right now, aroused, mussed from our lovemaking and enticed by the forbidden? Do I need to swing by the pharmacy first, though?"

Her brain filled with naughty images of James fucking her up the arse, it took her a minute to piece together what he meant. Pharmacy? Condoms. She blinked the heady lust out of her gaze and focused on him. Before, they'd both shared blood tests and had moved on from using protection. She was on the pill, and so there'd been no need.

They'd both been celibate in the interim, so she didn't see any issue from her perspective.

"I'm still on the pill," she assured him. "So I'm okay with us continuing where we left off."

James grinned, a devilish cast to his face that had her blood pumping faster.

"Well then," he murmured.

She shrieked as the hand that had been cupping her arse moved to spread her cheeks. He ran one finger over her tiny, puckered anus and caressed her right there. A million nerves sang to life, sensitive places and erogenous zones she hadn't even realized existed.

"I think —" A knock sounded at the door.

Instantly alert, El tensed as did James. El's muscles contracted, ready to spring into action. The ancient fight or flight instinct rode her hard. Rob's voice cut through the air and she relaxed. She felt the tension seep out of James as well. He wriggled his hands around her arse, as if finding a more comfortable hold. El's senses remained on alert, lust simmering just beneath the surface.

"El? Waldron's called. Are you all right in there? El?"

"Your bloody buggering partner and his poor sense of timing hasn't changed either." James sighed. He grinned wryly at her and El had to stifle a chuckle.

Rob's timing had been...interruptive a few times in the past.

"El?" Rob knocked harder on the door. His tone had raised and she knew if she didn't respond he'd start to worry.

Standing, it was only as her slacks started to slip down her hips that she recalled her state of disarray.

Decadent satisfaction and mild amusement instantly transformed into agitation.

"I can't answer the door like this," she said, somewhat horrified. Her fingers were sticky with James' juices. She was naked from the waist up, her pants unclasped. She didn't even want to consider the mess her hair must be or the small marks from their intimacy that would be over her body.

"Uh, just a second, Rob," she called out and raced to the sink. Turning the tap on, she washed her hands and scrubbed at her face, making certain the area around her mouth was clean. Even so, she feared Rob would take one look at her and spot something to indicate she'd just given an earth-shattering blow job to her thief.

Turning the tap off, she then got dressed super quickly. El rushed to where her bra and shirt were strewn and yanked them on. James still sat back on the couch, rumpled and mostly naked. El grinned at him even as she waved a hand at him to get up.

"You can't answer the door like that," she said in a hushed tone, hoping her partner couldn't hear through the door. Even though less than a minute had passed, Rob had been suspiciously quiet since she'd called out. Her partner was incredibly intelligent, and she didn't think it would take a rocket scientist to understand the delay. The longer it drew out, however, the more embarrassment she would suffer.

James stood and started righting his appearance. The lazy, satisfied glow, however, was not something he could just wipe off. Huffing out a soft laugh, El picked up her hair tie and ran her fingers through her long hair, pulling it back into a ponytail as she raced over to the door. Jerking it open, she tried to school her face into an innocent, vague look. Rob took one brief glance at her, then let his gaze slide past her to where James came up behind her.

"Waters," he nodded.

"Hey, Stevens, how've you been?"

"Oh, you know," Rob replied, "same old stuff. It's good to see you, though. We should catch up over a pint some other time."

Rob lifted a hand, waved his phone at her. The screen showed 'Waldron', indicating that her partner had just gotten a message from him. Rob's smile was sheepish.

"Look I know I'm interr—uh, Waldron just texted me a few more questions about the painting. James, can I ask you a few things about it?"

El turned, noted that James didn't have a clue what Rob meant but wasn't keen to show it.

"Erm, which particular painting do you mean?"

Rob glanced from James to her. He cocked an eyebrow and the teasing glint of humor shone in his eyes. She didn't need to see the cogs of his brain working at a crazy rate. She knew he was figuring the best way to tease her mercilessly over this. Despite the length of time she'd been inside, she hadn't even managed to get to the point of their visit—or the supposed point—and she knew she'd be paying dearly in taunts for weeks, if not months, to come.

Before Rob could even open his mouth to start the jokes and comments, she jumped in.

"I was getting to that, I swear. It was the next thing I was going to say when you knocked," she lied shamelessly. "What's Waldron found?"

"You know what?" Rob said smoothly as he pocketed his phone. "I can just do a quick search online. I don't need you to sit beside me and help with that. Why don't you stay here and...erm...*talk* with

Waters, explain the situation, and get back to me when you've plotted our next move? Don't hurry, though. I can cover for you, no problems."

"Rob." El took a small step forward, but her partner held out his hand in a stop motion.

He smiled at her, a warm, genuine grin.

"Don't, El. You've been miserable these last few months. This is the first time I've seen you happy, practically glowing. A few hours isn't going to make or break this case. I'll turn over a few stones. I can handle that on my own. Just..." Rob glanced from her to James, his grin widening though it was still friendly, not mocking. "Make sure you do actually explain the situation. I still think we could use the extra help."

"You're sure?" El scanned her colleague's gaze and posture. She didn't want to let him down, but the temptation to remain with James was strong. Nothing about Rob indicated that he was being anything other than completely truthful. She knew he wouldn't have offered to cover for her if he had doubts, but that didn't mean she took it lightly, either. She relaxed as she realized that Rob appeared more amused and pleased than annoyed at her unprofessional behavior.

"I'm sure. I'll catch up with you later." Rob lifted his hand and threw them a warm grin and quick wave.

"Do you think he was checking you were all right, or just giving you an out if we were screaming and shouting at one another?" James asked as they moved back into his flat and he pushed the door closed.

El chuckled.

"Probably a mixture of both. And," she added after a moment's pause, "possibly making certain I didn't need help burying your body. Knowing Robert, it's hard to guess how wild his imagination might have run."

"He'd help you bury a body?" James asked, hoping for clarification.

El tilted her head. He sounded surprised, but not upset. She nodded. "Sure, or I believe so. I know I'd help him if the situation was reversed."

She frowned in thought, studied James' face, relishing the fact she'd been given another chance with him. Reaching out, she then rubbed her fingertips across his stubble, enjoying the roughness of his morning growth.

"You know, I'd almost certainly help you clean up a messy murder too," she mused. "That way you smile at me, the blend of wicked and luscious, it makes me want to agree to anything you suggest, no matter how outlandish."

"Like anal intercourse?" he murmured, his voice thickening.

She wrapped her arms around him, hugged him tightly before she pulled back, forcing herself to take a couple of paces and put some distance between them.

Just those three words had her body humming, the need building within her once again. She swallowed and reminded herself that much as she'd love to drag him to bed and shag him silly, to let him plunder her body and do unspeakably pleasurable things, they *did* have a case to work.

"I'll put the kettle on, then we can sit down and I'll tell you a story," she said, ignoring the husky note to her voice.

Professional, she reminded herself. *You're a capable, rational woman. You don't need to jump his bones again… Or not yet, at least.*

"Give me five minutes," James agreed, his grin still deliciously wicked. "I'll grab a shower, change and we can get to work."

As he left the room she watched his arse with a wistful sigh. Part of her would love to share that shower with him, but she had a feeling if she did that then anal play would pop right back up and it would be days before they surfaced again.

Trying to force her mind off that enticing fantasy, she turned to get that tea started.

Chapter Four

"I must be further out of touch than I realized," James said two cups of tea later. "I haven't heard a thing about the National Gallery, or the stealing of that Cezanne. No wonder I had a dozen messages on my phone when I checked it after my shower."

"I hadn't thought of that." El sat forward in her chair. She'd decided not to sit next to James on the couch. The close proximity, coupled with the faint scent of sex still in the air, could tip her back out of her working mode. She placed her empty mug carefully on the floor, out of reach of where she might knock it over accidentally. "Will people think you had something to do with its theft? We might be able to work with that."

"I've only been dabbling over the last six to nine months," James reminded her with a wry grin. "While I'm far from reformed, I have been...perusing other paths, shall we say?"

"Oh?"

"A gorgeous red-haired spy has been instrumental in my reformation," he teased her.

She laughed.

"I'm still well in the game, but I've been very selective about the few jobs I've done. Using my skills for the greater good."

"I can't wait to get you over for dinner and ask more," she said.

"And I can't wait to have *you* for dinner, to lick and possess every last inch of that sinful body."

El closed her eyes for a moment and took a slow, steady breath. Huffing it out again, she shook her head. Not even wanting to go there, she changed the topic.

"I'm not surprised you're using your skills to help people. I've always known you were a good man, James. Even before we started seeing each other you never hurt anyone. You've never been a party to violence. I'm glad, though, that you're using your influence to assist others."

"I'm a thief and a criminal." While his tone was sharper than she'd expected, his blue eyes were cool and narrowed. "Don't paint me into being some misunderstood, tarnished hero."

"I wouldn't dream of it. Similarly, don't you try to blacken your character and expect me to believe you're some greedy, nefarious villain, either. You're a good man, James Waters. Stubborn, slippery and far too much of a bad influence on my professional focus, but an honest, reliable one nevertheless."

James stood, crossed over to her and perched on the arm of the chair she sat in. He bent down, then cupped her jaw in the palm of his hand. It was as if he were unable to resist the contact, like he needed it. El could sympathize, her hands itched to touch him too, but she forced herself to act in a restrained manner.

Allowing her face to be tilted up to him, she held his gaze in a silent mini battle of wills.

"Damn, but you're stubborn. Beautiful, miraculous, but so strong-willed I must be crazy," he commented.

There was no heat or anger in his tone, so she remained quiet, not needing to say anything. James leaned down and they kissed tenderly. She moaned, relaxing into it and loving the feel of his lips pressing to hers, the smooth way they tried to consume each other. She lifted a hand to touch his knee, needing that extra piece of contact with him as they explored each other's mouths.

All too soon he pulled back, sucking in a deep breath. He blew it out forcefully.

"And this isn't helping you recover the painting," he said with clear regret. "Okay, let's get back on topic. I can check my messages, see if anyone is contacting me about the heist. What else would you like me to do?"

"Get into their heads and try to wrap this all up. What remains of the team are either not of use or stonewalling us. Any data we collect could be critical. If this was your heist, your team, where would you have put the painting? They only had ninety minutes between escaping the Gallery and meeting at the docks. Two hours at most. That limits the area they could have used."

"Well if it had been my operation, there wouldn't be a team, for starters," James replied thoughtfully. "There has to be a reason Kent and Luke remained so hands on for this. Think about it logically—a team of five people going somewhere as high profile as the Gallery—that's madness. One person, two at most would be my plan. Particularly when these two idiots are smugglers by trade. Out of practice fences at that. They've been managers for a while, from what you've said. Why come along on this particular heist? It's not like they could add much to a smaller, more professional team. What made this heist, this painting, so special?"

El frowned, mentally replaying James' words. He had a point, a good one. She stood and looked around the room, her gaze partially internal as she continued to try to play the process out in her head.

"Do you have a computer? Or laptop? And paper? I need to make notes on this and check their files. I can log on to the work server remotely."

"Drag the coffee table closer to the couch," James said as he walked from the room. El spotted the table pushed against one wall and began rearranging the furniture. James returned with his arms full. Together they spent a few minutes setting everything up.

El logged into her work account and brought up the dossiers on the three members of the crew from the heist. Splitting the screen to show them all, she turned the laptop so James had a clear view.

"Fresh eyes never hurt. Give me your impressions."

James pulled the computer onto his lap and focused on reading. El started to jot down thoughts and ideas, mulling over the new angle James had given her. She wrote out Kent's and Luke's names on one side, Thaddeus, Chelsea and David in smaller letters beneath them, and created a kind of flow chart as her mind worked.

The shadowy figures of their clients, the Agency itself, and all the other parties involved in this heist, the Gallery and the painting itself she placed in the center of the page—center stage as the Cezanne appeared to be for this mission. The more detail she added into this chart, the more she came back to the painting. Its heist and subsequent auction was pivotal. El's gut was adamant on that.

Not wanting to let her own preconceptions cloud the scene, she continued to scribble notes, questions and facts. The chart grew as she did this. El racked her brain, putting everything she could recall into her chart. When she thought she'd finished, she ripped the page from the notepad and in small, neat lettering rewrote it clearly so she could look at the big picture.

Why would Kent and Luke have remained so involved in a complex, but straightforward heist? Sure, the National Gallery wasn't the average home invasion or small, independent store, but neither was it the Tower or protected like the Mint. More than the minimum necessary people didn't make sense.

Unless there was more than recovering the painting at stake?

Chelsea and David hadn't indicated that either man had a personal involvement with each other or Thaddeus, nor had there been time for them to contact anyone inside the Gallery itself. Chelsea had been their inside contact, and so had there been another connection somewhere she would have come across it.

It couldn't be personal—so it must be the painting itself. Could the painting be that critical? Or perhaps those whom they were selling it to were powerful enough that Kent and Luke felt the need to oversee everything personally, to micromanage the job.

No, that didn't fit properly. If they were afraid of their clients then they'd be scrupulous about the details and planning stage, but they wouldn't risk being caught because their team was too large.

The painting was key, it was the only logical answer. It felt right.

"What could make a painting so important that these guys would risk the potential success of the mission to keep tabs on it, to steal it personally?"

Her question, though spoken aloud, was partly rhetorical. She felt no offense when James looked up at her, but then returned his gaze to the screen of the laptop and continued scrolling.

"It wasn't ego," she continued as she stared at her flow chart. "Both men have plenty of that, but they're professionals. I can believe they'd be in on all the planning and behind the scenes stages, but they wouldn't have risked exposure by coming along into the Gallery itself. They're both physically strong and powerful in their smuggling circles, it doesn't fit they were scared of their clients. No, it was the painting. Maybe they wanted to steal it literally with their own hands, or maybe it's a talisman of some sort, a culmination of months of work. There's a reason for their actions. We find it, and maybe we'll find the painting."

El jolted when she glanced up to find that James had scooted closer to her on the couch and now peered over her shoulder, seeming intrigued by her complicated diagram.

"Can I see this?" he murmured.

She grinned, but handed it over. He scanned the document, appearing to take in the whole before analyzing individual areas more closely.

"I've never thought to map out a heist like this," he said without looking at her. "You've certainly captured the heart and many of the details. This is great."

James appeared enraptured. He pressed a finger to his lips, clearly studying the chart. She wondered if it felt like an intellectual challenge to him, to piece together the steps of who fitted where in relation to the painting. Happy for him to chew over it, she picked up the laptop and brought it to her legs, scanning through the documents, having read them multiple times before.

She let her eyes wander the screen, scrolling down as she needed. Not reading it per se, she let her subconscious mind fill in the blanks, hoping to pick out the important facts. James remained engrossed in the chart, distracted from his study of the crew. Tabbing over to Luke's dossier she remembered that he seemed to have been the brains behind the crew.

The ringleader, he'd hidden in plain sight, acting like the wing man for Kent, when in reality he'd been running the show all along.

"Luke was in charge," she said, more to herself than James. "It was never Kent's call, none of it was. Luke would have directed where they hid the painting. Somewhere close. Ninety minutes, even at that time of the evening, you can't drive far in central London."

Dimly she felt a frisson of energy, that tingle she often felt when a line tugged during an investigation connected with something. It felt right, solid. El returned to the top of the info pack and started to read carefully through the stats they had on Luke Calloway.

There, a dozen sentences in, was a list of his known kin.

He had a sister living in central London.

"Bullseye," she said, looking up and nudging James. "Louise Calloway, Luke's sister. She's in easy driving distance of the Gallery. Luke and Kent could have made the trip out to her place, left the Cezanne behind and been at the docks with plenty of time to spare."

James frowned, pursed his lips and seemed to think about it. A minute ticked by before he finally shook his head.

"I don't know, El. That doesn't sound right to me. Was there any indication Louise was involved in the smuggling?"

Uncertainty gnawed at her.

"No. No, I haven't seen anything that links her with that side of his business. And I know Luke called his lawyer, not Louise, after he was arrested. But look here," She pointed to the screen. "He's based primarily in Dublin. All his contacts, his mates, the vast majority of the real estate he owns is in Ireland. There's just a few scattered homes and warehouses along the coast of Wales and Scotland. There's no indication he has anything permanent or safe here in London. But his sister lives here. Surely that means something? Who else could he turn to, and trust, with this painting? It's logical, right?"

"I can see the logic," James admitted, "but why would he leave something this important with his sister? If she isn't a part of it… Well, it's not like he can just drop in unexpectedly, give her a hug and ask her to watch the priceless piece of artwork for him over a quick cup of tea before leaving again, is it?"

"I think it's worth asking her. Seeing her for ourselves and gauging her responses. It's an idea—a solid, actionable lead. Maybe the fact it isn't the smartest move for Luke to have made means it's too easy to overlook. Besides, she's family, and blood has to count for something, wouldn't you think?"

James tilted his head to the side, twisting his mouth as he thought about it. He nodded, placed her papers in a neat pile on the coffee table and stood.

"It doesn't have the zing of rightness for me, but that could be because we've only got part of the picture. It certainly can't hurt to speak with her."

Excitement sang through her blood. James had some good points, but they didn't have a better idea just now. Finding a thread, anything worth following, was always a step in the right direction. They'd moved her jacket to the floor when they'd set up the coffee table. El strode over and picked it up. She shrugged into it, then took her mobile phone from the inner pocket.

She checked her messages out of habit, finding her inbox empty.

"I'm just going to call Robert," she said. "Depending on how bored he is, or how badly he's driving everyone back at the office crazy, he might want to join us."

"I always wondered why the two of you didn't hook up," James said. He reached out, stroked his palm over her ponytail. El tilted her head slightly, enjoying the way James' touch felt. He had this knack of caressing his fingers over her hair and down the nape of her neck. It drove her wild and made her shiver delightfully.

"In some ways we're very similar," she had to drag her mind back to the task at hand. "We both enjoy putting the pieces together, solving the puzzle and finding answers. We work well together—after so many years, we're used to each other's rhythm and flow. I love him like my brother, though, and he feels the same in return. We're close, and there's a bond there—but it's platonic and I genuinely feel if we'd ever become sexually intimate we couldn't work the same together. That faith and trust we have would become…different. We'd lose focus and that would be harmful to the job."

"He's protective of you. I'm not poking at it. I think it's sweet and I can see he cares deeply about you. The two of you share something special and I'd not change that."

"We're protective of each other," she agreed. "He's strong and almost scarily intelligent. Rob... How can I explain it? He thinks on a different line to everyone else, almost non-linear. Sometimes he'll put things together in a manner I never in a billion years would have thought of, but then something that is right in front of his nose, something every single human with an IQ over forty can comprehend, he will be completely blind to."

"Really?" James looked stunned.

El chuckled.

"He has this friend, Sally... They're both deeply in love and he can't see it—he doesn't even fully grasp the fact he adores her, and he'd never believe me if I explained she loved him in return. I'm determined to open his eyes, but things have been crazy lately."

"He's lucky to have such a caring partner like you."

"I'm glad to have him too. Sometimes Rob can be a handful, especially when he gets the bit between his teeth. He went through a number of partners before we were paired up. I think Waldron was relieved when we got along so well. Now I have a feeling if either of us requested another partner—something that management is supposed to respect if anyone wishes for a change—we'd be denied and they'd move heaven and earth to keep us together. Not that we'd ever ask for it. It sounds conceited, but we kick arse together. We're a good fit, professionally speaking."

James grinned.

El slipped her phone into the pocket of her pants and wrapped her arms around his waist. She drew her body flush against his and stood up on her toes. Brushing her lips lightly over his, she teased them both, taunted him with her soft skin. She flicked her tongue out and licked his lips, moistening them.

He opened his mouth to her and she probed inside, loving the taste of him. The kiss slowly deepened between them. Passion heated her blood and a knot of desire grew in her belly. She roamed her hands over his back, lowering until she cupped his arse and pulled his hips into hers. As she ground into his crotch, her breath caught. She was turning herself on as much as him. El rubbed herself along his thickening length.

"You need to make that call," he said, his voice husky with growing need.

El drew in a deep breath, opened her eyes and caught his gaze. She smiled. "I guess I do," she agreed. Reluctantly she pulled her phone back out and dialed Rob's number. He answered after only two rings.

"Stevens."

"Rob, it's El. How's it going?"

"I'm drowning over here, how are you? Is everything all right?"

"It's perfect." She couldn't keep the satisfaction from her voice. There was a pause as her gaze clashed with James'. Lust sparkled in his eyes and for a moment she imagined herself dumping the case, stripping naked, locking the door and performing every imaginable wicked act on and with the sexy man before her.

Rob cleared his throat and she was reminded of his presence.

"Um. I'm calling because I think we should talk to Louise Calloway. She might know something, or if we're lucky, Luke could have left the Cezanne with her."

"Neither Chelsea nor David ever reported Calloway contacting his sister," Rob said, sounding distracted. She heard papers being shuffled and guessed he was sifting through the file, looking for the other agents' reports.

"I know, but it seems stupid to ignore such an obvious connection. I didn't want to rush off and leave you in the lurch, though. Do you want to meet us there?"

"Hmm. Will James be going with you?"

El lifted an eyebrow, even though her partner couldn't see it.

"Yes, why?"

"I think the two of you should pursue that line of inquiry," Rob said formally.

"Waldron has come close?" she guessed.

"That's correct. Yes. Hang on... Right, he was just walking past. Look, El, you've obviously, erm, kissed and made up. I don't want to barge in. Waldron has me trying to source rumors about the Cezanne. If you come back here you'll be snowed under with paperwork. I'm hoping to escape in an hour or so, but for now I think your time is better spent with James. Enjoy being with him. I like seeing you happy, and he's obviously a big part of that. This might turn into one of those times where splitting us up and one partner covering for the other means we can close the case."

"Like the Renfield one?" she recalled.

Sometimes — rarely — management found themselves with a sensitive, political, messy case. When such things weren't neat and straightforward, even the normal amount of freedom and leeway became restricted as pressure came from all sides. In the past, El and Rob had dealt with it by one of them going out and doing the hard work while the other one shuffled papers and kissed up to Waldron, or whoever was pressuring them to wrap the case up in a specific way.

Considering the amount of political fallout the attack on the Gallery and loss of the Cezanne must be generating, El wasn't surprised that Waldron was riding Rob hard.

"You'll escape soon, though, right? I don't want you carrying the weight here. We're partners. James understands that. If you need a break, or for us to swap over and for me to come in, I'm trusting you to let me know, Rob."

"Of course. Besides, I've been thinking of doing some interviews — stuff Waldron will be okay with. I just need to wrap up our preliminary report here then I'll be clear. If those interviews fall through, I'll think of something, anything to get me out there trying to answer these questions. Don't worry about me, follow your instincts. And warn James to rein you in if you get into any trouble."

"I never get into trouble," she protested.

James choked out a laugh and she shot him a heated, sensual look.

Rob chuckled on the other end. "Right. You're the hot-headed one around here, remember?"

She laughed and had to give him that point, but she'd not bend over that easily.

"If I recall, *you're* the last one who threw a dozen case files to the floor in a fit of frustration."

"And it was you who almost got us both on archiving duties for life when you decked that idiot manager... What was his name? Thompson? Johnson?"

"Thomasson," El agreed. "But that bastard deserved it. Everyone agreed. Eventually."

They shared a laugh.

"Okay," El said. "James and I will go talk to Louise. You get out from under that paperwork as quickly as you can manage. I'll fill you in later."

"Be safe," he said.

"You too."

She hung up then placed her phone back in her jacket pocket.

"Rob's kissing arse and covering for us. Let's go squeeze Louise gently and see what we can find."

"I'll drive us. Do you have the address?"

El nodded. She watched while James walked around the small room mumbling about his keys, wallet and phone. In a few minutes they were at the door, locking it and heading for his small car.

She felt the normal thrill of the hunt, pleased to be out and doing something and not stuck at her desk shuffling paper like poor Rob was. Better still, she felt lighthearted, pleased in a way she hadn't been for months. It took her a minute, but she realized that the feeling stemmed from having James there with her.

He unlocked her door and held it open. Instead of climbing in, she cupped his jaw, tugged him down and kissed him thoroughly. They were both breathing heavily when he pulled back, and her eyes had lost focus. She cleared her throat and collected herself, needing a moment to calm her racing heart and blink to bring herself back from the sensual haze he'd taken her into.

"What was that for?" James asked.

"I'm glad you're here, that we're doing this together."

He grinned wickedly at her and grabbed her arse lightly, giving it a teasing squeeze.

"I'll take payment later. But, being honest, I'm getting a thrill from it. I've never played the good guy in this situation. I've always been on the other end. It's interesting to see how this side works."

El pressed a kiss to his cheek. "Careful you don't enjoy it too much," she warned with a laugh. "You might be corrupted and end up joining the side of light after all. Think of how ruined your reputation as an internationally acclaimed thief would be then, if it got out you were assisting our Agency and the forces of good?"

James shuddered in mock horror. "I don't think I could bear it."

"I could make it worth your while," she purred as she stroked his jaw and nipped a few biting kisses along its length. James breathed heavily. She pressed a palm over his chest and felt his heart pounding. He seemed turned on by the thought.

Pleased she'd come out on top of that minor skirmish, El turned and climbed into the passenger seat. It took him a minute to regain control of himself, but James slammed the door and came around to the driver's seat. As he started the car and they pulled away from the curb she realized the silence between them was charged with a thick, heavy sexual chemistry.

She didn't mind it in the least.

Chapter Five

"Could you please lower that badge a little? I can't see it clearly."

El opened the small leather folder more and lowered it as requested. Louise Calloway's door had only been opened the slightest crack, and a shadow was the only indication that a person stood there. El tried to decide if Louise was paranoid, or perhaps had gone through this routine enough times to want to follow the very letter of procedural law. It wasn't common for her to be asked to show her badge, though she was willing to comply. Perhaps Louise had been attacked by someone using this routine, it wasn't for her to judge.

"I've never heard of the Department of Special Research," Louise said.

"It's a small branch, ma'am," El replied. She kept holding the badge and laminated identification card out, though her instinct was to replace it. "I can give you a phone number to call, to verify my badge number, name and department. But we just have a few questions for Louise Calloway regarding her brother. They're completely standard. You're not in any trouble, ma'am."

"I suppose so," Louise sighed and opened the door. El regarded her.

Only of medium height, maybe five foot five, Louise was reed thin. A somewhat faded house dress of dark green was warmly covered by a thickly knitted blue cardigan. Her brown hair was pulled back tightly into a French braid. Louise looked tired, as if over the years life had beaten her up. She stood up straight, met El's and James' eyes as she stepped back and allowed them entrance into her small flat.

El felt that, even though Louise looked as though she'd been hammered by the world, she still had plenty of pride. The woman was not defeated or broken down. That took strength. El respected her for it. Taking a quick look around the room, she saw that Louise didn't outwardly appear to live above her means. The living room was small. Two couches sat at right angles to create a small sub-section with a TV and stereo system. A comfortable-looking chair sat beside the window with a large lamp in what appeared to be the perfect reading, knitting or stitching corner.

The room was warm, lived in, but showed few personal effects. El got the feeling that Louise liked her privacy and was not one to share. This instinct was backed up by the fact that the woman didn't chatter nervously. Louise met El's eyes and the three of them remained standing in the room.

"You can't look around," Louise stated. "Unless you have a warrant, which you should have already shown me. I know my rights. You said this was about Luke, what's happened?"

"Ma'am, your brother was involved with the incident that occurred at the National Gallery. Please understand we're trying to keep the worst of these details out of the media—I'd appreciate it if you don't pass on what we're about to discuss. Your brother and some of his team members have been involved in the attack on the Gallery and stolen a painting. Do you know anything about this?"

Louise shook her head, her lips thinning in a pinched manner. Her mouth became drawn into an unhappy frown. El saw the moment the woman hit upon the notion to deny it. Her eyes lightened somewhat and a few of the wrinkles on her brow eased. El thought it was very telling that Louise's first, gut instinct was to believe her brother capable of it. Innocent people usually denied first and only came around after.

"That's not Luke's style," Louise insisted. "From what I've heard on the news, they suspect terrorists. There were rocket launchers and a coordinated attack. I've seen footage of the Gallery, it's a shambles. They're saying it will take millions of pounds to reconstruct the outer façade alone."

"And that isn't your brother's style?" El questioned.

Louise shook her head impatiently. "My brother has been a part of his fair share of destruction, Officer. But it's a rare occurrence his plans reach the news, and international coverage at that. He's too smart and subtle for that level of mess. Coverage means attention, and in his business that sort of notice isn't needed. Word of mouth, gossip, rumors, those are what he aims for. He needs people to talk about his work, for the knowledge to spread, but having groups of outraged citizens baying for his blood, to have rich, powerful people want to destroy him, is way out of his range."

El nodded and cast a quick glance to James. When she and Rob interviewed people, they often had a smooth, easy rhythm going. He caught her look and seemed to understand that she felt it was time for him to add to the conversation. Only she would have recognized the fleeting glance of worry that crossed his face. James promptly covered it, smoothed his features so he once again looked like a sober, serious professional.

"Uh, that fits the same sort of thing we thought," he said a little awkwardly.

Louise turned to face him for the first time.

James held up well under her intelligent glare. El noticed that he even managed to appear sympathetic. She had to hide her smile. He was playing good cop, she decided.

"You see, Miss Calloway, the risks for your brother and his team were quite high. This was a complicated, intricate project they'd undertaken. There must have been a powerful reason behind your brother wanting to do this. Can you think of why he could have been driven to this? Did he hold a grudge against the Gallery? Or was he obsessed with any particular painting? Or artist? Any information you can give to us would be helpful, please."

A part of her wondered if he'd ever considered working for the Agency. James looked sincere in his desire for illumination. El bet with seasoning and practice, James could coax bloody secrets out of a stone maiden. The fact that he was charming, sexy and flat out gorgeous didn't hurt either. What better way to seduce women out of their knickers than for a handsome rogue to offer them sympathy and understanding?

Louise's body language softened to James. Obviously the woman was not immune to his charms, either.

"I've not been close with my brother since we were children," she said. "I'm fairly sure when we were small we had the usual school visit to the Gallery. He probably went there once, maybe twice in our youth. I also am not going to lie about the fact he loves artwork, pretty and expensive things. But it's the money, the power and prestige that comes with these things he enjoys. The artworks themselves are just objects to him. Wealth, power and standing—those are the idols my brother craves."

"He's never mentioned specific paintings to you? Pieces of art? Or even favorite artists? Monet, Degas, Cezanne, Renoir?" James pressed lightly.

El remained silent and eased very slowly a half step back, giving her lover the floor. Pride welled in her for his skill and the fast way he read Louise's character and used this knowledge.

She'd never thought of James as a pretty face, or just a lovely piece of arse. Watching him work, though, was delightful. In the darkest part of her soul, she wondered briefly what it would be like to run a con with him. She imagined the thrill it would be to break in somewhere illegally and touch priceless artefacts, jewels, and see paintings and sculpture in some rich person's private stash that few, if any, people ever got to lay eyes on.

El had never denied understanding the thrill that could come with such actions, but she also could see the bigger picture. And therein lay her clay feet. While she could well understand and even imagine the addictive thrill breaking and entering could give, and touching with her bare hands priceless jewels and *objets d'art*, the price of a single misstep was too high for her.

"No," Louise said with a shake of her head. "I'm sorry. Mostly it was what things like that could give him he craved. Not the items themselves. Are you sure it's him? He's been in Ireland since he left school. He hated London, detested what it reminded him of. We exchange cards for Christmas and our birthdays, and I get the odd phone call from him, but we haven't really kept in touch. I'd have thought if he were here in London he'd contact me."

James caught El's glance, and she read his look. He wanted to pass the ball back to her.

"We're certain it's him, ma'am," El spoke in a soft tone. "He's not denied being a party to the heist, nor has he cooperated in letting us know where he and his partner hid the painting."

"Cooperated?" Louise repeated. She looked from El to James then settled her gaze back on El. "You have my brother in custody? Here in London?"

Shifting uncomfortably on the inside, El didn't let anything outwardly show. She held Louise's gaze and spoke the truth. "Yes. He's been arrested."

"Wait. Why wasn't I informed of this? If he's been detained then I should be his contact, as his next of kin. What kind of game are you people playing? Where is he? I want to see him, right now."

"He was given his phone call, as is the law, ma'am. I believe he called his lawyer. That was his choice and his right. We're not playing anything. As I stated, we're here to ask you about Luke Calloway and hopefully ascertain where he stashed the painting he stole from the National Gallery."

"I don't know anything about that," Louise insisted. She crossed to a slender cupboard beside the door, opened it and removed a scarf and coat. "Look, the last time I spoke with Luke, he was busy. I know what that usually means and I don't ask. I love my brother, but we're not on particularly close terms. I've answered your questions to the best of my ability and I have no clue where the bloody painting or anything else is. Now, I want to go and see my brother, please."

The clear agitation in Louise's movements as she jerkily pulled on her coat and wrapped the scarf around her neck told its own story. She was surprised that Luke was in town and shocked he'd been arrested. She also appeared to have had no clue that he was a part of the Gallery heist. El's instincts said she genuinely knew little to nothing about the entire deal.

Had Louise told them every scrap of information she had? Probably not. But El felt sure the woman knew nothing about the painting or its current whereabouts. James and Rob had been right—it wasn't here. El still felt as though this had been needed. Pursuing all leads meant there was no chance of overlooking something, or missing a connection. It was time consuming, but thorough. They hadn't wasted the trip.

Investigative work, she'd learned from Rob and her own experience, was analyzing and following through every thread until they finally found a hot one and unraveled it to see the whole story. That meant they often spent a good portion of their time talking to people and seeking knowledge that ended up meaning little or nothing.

El dug her badge and identification card out again, opened it and pulled a business card from the small fold in the leather wallet.

"I haven't been back for a few hours — it's possible they've moved your brother since I last saw him," she said. While El didn't want to be too vague, and she certainly didn't want to lie to Louise, neither was she keen to have the woman storm the doors of the Agency if it wasn't necessary. She turned the card over as she pulled a pen from the pocket of her jacket. In small, neat script she wrote the main switchboard number that was manned day and night.

"Call this number, say you've spoken with Eleanor Williams and are Luke Calloway's sister. The receptionist will know the case you're referring to and either be able to answer your questions, or put you in contact with whoever is currently in charge of the custody of your brother."

El handed the card to Louise, who took it and stared at it as though it was a viper about to poison her or sink fangs into her fingers.

"Is he in danger?" Louise asked, her voice sounding small and scared.

El felt sympathy for the woman. Clearly she'd not had an easy life, but she'd done what she could. El hoped her brother didn't drag her down with him now.

"Legally, he's in it up to his neck," El said with as much kindness as she could. "The case against him is rock solid. He had the painting in his possession less than two hours before he was apprehended and now is refusing to return the stolen item or cooperate with the authorities... It's not the way to gain leniency. On top of that there are a number of questions we have about the painting and its importance..." El shrugged, not wanting to divulge too much more in case Louise was playing a very deep game and was about to repeat everything back to Luke.

"Physically, no, he's not in danger from us. I can't answer that for where he's heading, of course. But legally, yes. He is in very hot water. I'm sorry."

Louise nodded and opened the door for them.

"Thank you," she said, a small wave of the card indicating what she spoke of. "I'm sorry to push you out, but I want to see my brother."

"Of course," El said. She and James left the flat and remained silent as they walked out onto the street.

Thrusting her hands into her pockets, she looked back. There was no indication that Louise was watching them from the window, but with sheer curtains giving the flat privacy, if she were smart there wouldn't be a giveaway of her presence. El started walking back to their car, keeping her own counsel until they were out of sight of Louise's home.

"What do you think?" El asked, genuinely curious about his thoughts.

"She didn't know he was here," James replied. "Her surprise at that was true. As was her shock at him being arrested. I think she was a bit peeved we played her—asked our questions before telling her he was in custody—but she's sharp. It will only take a minute or two of thought for her to understand we knew she'd not say a word if she knew we had Calloway in the interview room."

El nodded. "That's how I read it too. I also think she was being truthful about having no knowledge of the whereabouts of the painting. Even so, there was something there. She didn't seem surprised he'd gone after the artwork, or the important pieces. When she talked about the power of such artwork, their prestige... I don't know, something clicked for me. She knew there were items out there that had meaning for Luke. She's not a complete innocent in all this, though I suspect she's been largely kept out of it."

"I agree. I also think she's been in closer touch with Calloway than she admitted to. She seemed to know the broad strokes of what he does. She wasn't indignant or righteous enough to be genuinely estranged from him."

"I'll note that in my report," El said.

James unlocked his car and opened the door for her.

"Thanks," she said as she climbed in. James came around and sat in the driver's seat. Only as he pulled away did she continue, "The main thing we need to do is find that damn painting, but it's important to also note Louise Calloway might have more knowledge than she's letting on. We can pump her if it comes to that, pressure her to spill what she knows, but I think that will be general knowledge of Calloway and his smuggling ring, his day-to-day operations. I think she's fairly out of the loop when it comes to the Cezanne."

"Which again leads us to the question of what's so special about this damn painting? Why is it so different? Calloway has broken almost every rule and protocol he's lived by — very successfully — this last dozen or more years. We find what it is about this damn piece that's so entrancing and we'll have practically wrapped the case up."

El cast him a laughing glance. James appeared as enthralled as she with the questions, the puzzle.

"You're loving this," she teased him. He shot her a hot, lusty glance. The look in his eyes had her blood pumping and heart racing. She craved to push his seat back, climb into his lap and forget everything else around them. Part of her couldn't believe the depth of effect he had on her. One searing gaze and she burned for him, yearned to feel him thrusting inside her.

"Something like that," he murmured in response, though she could barely remember the words she'd just spoken.

El wasn't fooled by the deceptively mild tone of his voice. She'd bet a week's pay he was thinking about doing something wicked. It was in his satisfied smirk, the hungry way he roamed his eyes over her body and the spark she saw in his gaze. She couldn't blame him either. Mental pictures of him spreading her ass open, touching her tiny hole and pushing his thick, slick cock into her hidden depths kept distracting her, too.

Shaking her head, El blew out an aggravated huff.

"So we're back to where we started," she sighed.

James changed gears as the car picked up speed, then moved his hand to press her thigh warmly. "You said once, when I asked how you could not be driven mental by all the dead ends you must come across, that a dead end simply gives you a thread to snip off and know it wasn't part of the package. Louise Calloway, while she might be worth questioning further later, is one of those."

"I know," El replied. She tried to keep the miffed tone out of her voice at having her words repeated back to her. "But the longer the Cezanne is missing, the more chance there is that others will find it. Hell, without proof that Calloway, Phillipe and Brown were a party to stealing it, we might end up having the charges against them reduced. Just between us, it also burns me that we can't seem to find a reason for any of this either. What the hell is it with this painting? I'm annoyed I can't seem to see the big picture here. Maybe—"

"When was the last time you ate?" James cut in.

El's instinct was to snap at him, but she pressed her lips closed before she did so. Hunching her shoulders, she realized what her lover was doing. She was working herself up. Getting aggravated would not help her solve this case. Temper would dull her instincts, and she needed every advantage possible.

El took a deep breath, forced herself to settle down. She threw a small, reluctant smile at James, silently acknowledging that his point was correct and she understood.

"I had a half stale Danish and crappy Agency coffee a little after three a.m. when Rob and I were first called in on the case. Oh, and I had some very good tea at your flat earlier," she said, fairly certain she knew where he was heading with this. There was no surprise when James threw her a baleful look. She smiled impishly in return.

"And you wonder why you're getting short-tempered? Frustrated? It's long past time you should have eaten. I'd prefer if we went back to my place. You can have full run of the laptop and work remotely, surely. I'm not keen to join you in that tiny room you call a flat."

This time it was she who cast him a murderous glance.

"I do little but sleep at my flat," she returned sharply. "And it's a ten minute Tube ride to work. It suits me perfectly."

"We'll be lucky if we can both breathe on that spindly couch you've used some sort of magic to fit in there. If we go back to my place, I'll get you some lunch from the deli around the corner."

Pride had El rebuffing almost before the words had finished leaving James' mouth. She hesitated once she had heard the offer fully out.

James' local deli was amazing. They had these homemade, sundried tomatoes that the owner's wife added a dash of chili to. Marinated for weeks in a secret recipe, they melted and sang on her tongue. The owner must have sold a portion of his soul for his cold meats connection, too. He always had the best stuff, freshly available. And his brie... Her mouth watered in remembrance.

"They've started stuffing their own olives," James added, seeming to read her mind as her silence lengthened in memory. El turned to look at him. Despite the fact that he was studying the road with far more concentration than strictly necessary, he couldn't hide the twitch of a smile. Evidently feeling the weight of her gaze, he stole a quick glance at her, the grin breaking out over his face. It lightened his face, made him appear young, devastatingly handsome and charming.

El's heart thudded.

She loved this man. Desperately so. With a burning intensity hotter than the fires of Hades and far more consuming.

"I'm not a cheap date," she capitulated. "It'll cost you some pastrami, spiced salami, those sundried tomatoes they make, a small tub of these olives you're tempting me with and their double brie. I'll grab some sour dough bread if the bakery is still next door?"

"It is, and you're cheap for that price," James said.

She chuckled and rested her hand over his on the gear stick. "You know me too well," she said.

"You'd be able to tempt me just as easily if the roles were reversed."

El laughed. "Food would be second on your list. If you were in a bitch of a mood like I just was, I'd be offering you kinky sexual favors. Or not even offering, but just doing. There was no one in the vicinity when we got into the car. I'd have just pushed your seat back, climbed into your lap and—"

"Fuck, I'm going to crash the car if you say another word," James swore as he swerved the wheel.

El looked at him and smirked, her point thoroughly made. He glanced back at the road a few times, his focus almost fully upon her. He laughed after a moment, tilting his head to give her that point.

"Holy shit, you've more than adequately made it clear you know me well, too. Let's not become one more road statistic, though."

El licked her lips and managed to stay silent for another minute.

"I was thinking about that when we got into the car earlier, anyway. But I got distracted thinking I'd rather have you ream my arse. That would prove rather difficult to do in here, though. Then I got back to thinking about this baffling case and my mood understandably soured."

James glanced at her a few more times. She chuckled, lifted her hand away from his, not trusting herself to have much more contact with him just yet, and waved at the road.

"Better focus on that. I'd like to make it back to your flat in good health. I think we both have plans for later."

"Bloody right on that," he muttered.

Feminine power had her feeling almost drunk. Her frustrations seemed negligible just now. They were still present, simmering under the surface, but they no longer consumed her. Heat flooded her body. Desire, liquid and potent, had her pussy slick and her nipples tight.

Oh yeah, she had plans for herself and James. While some of them included finding this damn painting and getting answers, others were far more sensual and provocative in nature.

James drove like a man possessed, his features hard and controlled. It didn't take a psychic to realize his mind was consumed with delicious, wicked thoughts of what waited for them when they got back to his flat.

Chapter Six

"You've called Robert Stevens. Please leave a message and I'll get back to you."

Beep.

"Rob, it's El. Just a heads up for you—Louise Calloway is likely headed into HQ to check on her brother. Neither James nor I think she's involved in this, though I do believe she knows more than she's told us about the work he does in general. I gave her my card and the main reception number we give out to civilians. I'll call you back when I know more. Be safe."

Snapping her phone closed, she pondered for a moment the reasons why Rob mightn't be answering his mobile phone. She debated calling the landline at his desk, but decided she might just be acting paranoid. Rob was a grown man and more than capable of not getting himself in over his head. With his height, strength and physical capabilities, there were few men who could take him on, one on one.

"Everything all right?" James asked as he entered the living room carrying two plates piled with enormous sandwiches. El took a deep breath, pushed the stupid concern away and smiled.

"Yes. I left a message, he didn't answer the call."

James set the plates on the coffee table but didn't sit. She could feel the tenderness and concern as he studied her features. He remained silent. Not wanting to spread her stupid concerns, El smiled. She reached out and touched James' arm.

"He's probably driving, or talking with someone about the case, and can't stop to answer his phone. He knows I'd have texted him with our emergency signal if something was wrong, so if he was busy and saw my number he'd not necessarily answer. I'm not going to worry. Not yet."

James nodded, accepting her explanation. Reaching his hands up, he then cupped her shoulders, drawing her into his embrace. El relaxed, her body melting into his. She held him tightly, soaking up the warmth emanating from his chest.

"I've missed you," she murmured, lifting her chin to stare at him. For the hundredth time she memorized his features, willing herself to impress his face in her mind so she'd never forget a thing.

"Me too," he replied.

James lowered his head and they kissed. It started out simply, almost chaste. Every time she experienced this, the wonder never dissipated. His lips were so soft, so perfect. She could die a happy woman if she never kissed another soul except this man. El tugged on his shirt, lifting it from the waistband of his pants. His skin was warm to her touch.

She moaned with approval. Smooth and hard, the flat planes of his muscled chest were delicious and she enjoyed the sensation of them under her hands. El traced her fingers up the small notches of his back, paying particular attention to the indentation of his spine. James shivered, growling huskily as they continued to parry and thrust their tongues together. She knew he was particularly sensitive there—it was why she focused her attention on the straight, long line of his backbone.

Passion grew through her body. She moved her mouth hungrily over his. He started to remove her clothes and the air filled with small sounds of pleasure from them both. Heat fused them together. It was only the beginning stages. She knew they'd burn before they sated each other.

"Off," El panted as she tugged his shirt up over his head. "Get it all off."

Shoes, pants and clothes were stripped off. El thrust her breasts forward as she arched back to remove her bra.

"Damn you're gorgeous," James breathed.

Distracted, El threw him a naughty, ravenous look over her shoulder. He was naked and breathtakingly erect. Her gaze heated, roamed down the long, muscular, perfect length of him.

James bit off a curt cuss and closed the distance between them. Standing there with her breasts pressed forward, and in her lacy thong, El didn't have the brainpower—nor the urge—to move as he dipped, pressed his shoulder to her stomach and slung her over his body in a fireman's carry.

Arse waving in the air, blood rushing to her head, her long red hair falling in her face and down in front of her, she could only laugh.

"James? Wait. What are you—?"

He lightly slapped her bum, a tiny sting that further aroused her. Not the sort of girl to remain placid—even when at a disadvantage—El worked her arms behind her and unclasped her bra. She tossed it to the floor as James entered the bedroom. Hooking her fingers into the waistband of her thong she tried to remove that too, but lost her grip as he lowered her to the bed.

She held her palms out to brace her descent. James' warm body quickly followed her down. He flipped her onto her back and she grinned wickedly at him. He skimmed the tiny triangle of lace down her legs. His hunger visible on his face, James reached back up. He pressed his palms to her inner thighs, exerted a small force and coaxed her to spread for him.

Eagerly, she complied.

"Fuck but I've missed this," James' tone was rough, but his touch was exquisitely gentle.

El bent her elbows on the mattress and lifted her head and chest up to watch. Her lover lay between her legs, his face level with her pussy. Gently, he placed a hand under her arse, cupped her and lifted as he simultaneously lowered his head and licked a long, wet line along her lips.

The warmth of his tongue seared her. Tingles of pleasure followed the trail he made. El dug her heels into the bed, tilted higher and pressed forward, urging him on. Not needing any more incentive, James grasped her hips, angled her to his liking and ate at her.

Shocking sensations rippled through her. His tongue was devious, naughty and deliciously teasing. He spread her lips, devoured her with a hungry passion that couldn't be faked. When he stroked over her clit, she arched up from the bed, crying out. Hands shaking, her breaths came faster, her heart beating so fast she felt it would break from her chest. Knots of delicious tension grew in her belly and still he pushed her higher. James joined his fingers with his tongue, and El had to fall back to the bed, her eyes pressed shut against the intensity that buffeted against her.

El gasped—the sounds that fell from her lips now couldn't be put into words. The noise was raw, earthy and elemental. James pumped into her, seeking and finding every nerve and tender place and using that knowledge to devastating effect.

Hot, slick pressure pushed against her anus. A fire of nerves burned at his touch. El cried out in bliss, her body moving without her conscious will. Looking down, she saw James watching her, and her face flushed hotly. His lips glistened with her juices as he continued to lick and suck at her.

"James," she moaned, caught up in the whirling vortex he'd created.

She felt his finger press at her puckered rear entrance. Her body resisted. He moved his hand and he collected more of her cream before returning again. The slick sensation was divine, even though she understood he was using it to grease his way. Slowly but with a steady force, he eased the tip of his finger into her anal passage.

Pressure turned to pain. Need blurred with resistance.

Logically, El knew full well that James' cock could fit inside her arse. Men and women performed this act every day. Sensible reason, however, didn't mean much when the mere tip of his finger had her feeling like her backside was on fire.

"I don't think—" El bit off the words, tried to breathe through the discomfort. James didn't lift his head from her pussy, so he could only mumble encouragingly. He shifted his free hand, tilting her hips down slightly to let him lick her clit in slow, wet circles.

Pleasure fought against the pain and the line blurred once again. El opened herself to the growing sensations, dizzy from the overwhelming dichotomy she'd never experienced before. Time dropped away and it was as if she and James were in their own little bubble. Nothing else mattered. Just him. His finger. Those feelings he could bombard her with.

All too soon, El found herself pressing her buttocks backward, accepting more of his digit. James balanced her perfectly, adding more sweetness when his possession became too much to bear. His progress was slow, but he had patience and seemed to enjoy watching her discover this new boundary.

When her body sang once again, he lifted his head. Overwhelming need had her uncaring at the loss of stimuli.

"El, darling, I need to get the lube."

She nodded, beyond speech. El didn't initially understand why he'd said this, until he carefully removed the finger up her arse, stroking her from the inside. The loss of that penetration had her gasping with dismay. She lowered her hand, then stroked her clit and played with one breast. She didn't want to lose this moment.

James moved quickly, opening the bedside drawer and removing a tube, returning seconds later. He rested his eyes on her, pleasuring herself, splayed decadently on his bed. His gaze was admiring as he appeared to soak the sight up. When their eyes met, she grinned at him, wanton and not the least shy about it.

"Roll over, darling," he murmured. "Let me prepare your arse. Damn you're a gorgeous sight."

Bracing a palm flat on the bed, El continued to caress her clit as she rolled onto her knees. Looking over her shoulder, she watched as James coated his thick, hard cock with the gel, then added more to his fingers until they shined with the slickness. She almost didn't feel the slender digit slide a few inches into her arse, it was so well greased.

Only as he added a second finger did the pressure return. She widened her knees, lifted her arse and concentrated on relaxing her muscles.

"I've imagined this countless times," he confessed. "Next time I'd love to restrain you, bind you to the headboard, maybe even spank you first. Redden your delicious arse to compliment the contrast between your pale skin and fiery hair. Damn, you're every fantasy I could wish for, El."

Turning, she gazed at him over her shoulder.

"If we're going to get kinky then you'd better expect to indulge in a few of my fantasies too. I've always wanted to dabble with a cock ring. See how far I can push those boundaries of yours."

He lifted one dark blond eyebrow. James seemed intrigued but not turned off by her suggestion. He nodded once.

"Seems like we have plenty to discuss later. I can handle that, El. It sounds tempting."

James continued to caress his fingers within her inner passage, stretching her. El kept the pressure on her clit, blending the opposing sensations until she could hardly breathe through the strength of her need.

"Fuck me, James," she panted, pleading with him. "I need more. Please."

"It'll be my pleasure," he replied, his voice strained.

El groaned as James widened his fingers inside her, opening her even more as he slowly withdrew. She felt hollow, destitute when he left her. Glancing back at him, she watched James, entranced by the fierce look of concentration on his face. At first she didn't understand what the pressure at her opening was. It felt alien, indescribable.

Pressure bloomed into pain. She cried out, shocked more than actually hurt.

"Wait," James murmured. "Bloody hell, you're so tight, like a clamping vice around my cock." He didn't appear to be speaking to her, but rather himself. He was focused completely on his actions.

Fierce, potent pleasure seared her. She gasped, her body feeling under attack. James played his fingers deliciously over her skin and found every erogenous zone from her pussy back to her open anal passage. Swamped with the sensations, she could only wriggle her behind at him in delight, groaning with approval.

"More," she pleaded as she shifted back to accept another tiny thrust from his shaft.

"That's the right note. Sing for me, baby," James crooned to her.

Hunger built within her as his cock slid slowly deeper. El reached between her spread thighs and stroked her clit. It only took a few slick swipes to take the edge off the pain of his possession. Eased into the sensation of his thick length piercing her rear, El found she couldn't distinguish fully between what hurt and what didn't. The blurring emotions jolted her system. With surprise, she found herself pressing her hips backwards, pushing her body to impale itself deeper on his cock.

This time they both moaned, caught up in the heat.

"James," she panted, unable to articulate anything further.

"El," he replied, seeming to be as caught up as she.

"Harder," she pleaded. "Please, fuck me harder. Right now."

"Bossy wench," James' voice was husky and deep, but the words were a caress, not annoyed.

He took her at her word. He grasped her with his warm hands, held tightly to her hips, pulled her up and back as his shaft sank completely within her. Tingles shot up her spine as inner nerves were brushed by his rock-hard erection. They were both panting hard. El felt sweat bead down her spine as her heart pounded as though it would explode.

James withdrew and pressed back inside her, thrusting his cock deeply into her arse like a man possessed. The burning intensity of his penetration, the overwhelming pleasure and pain at the incredible intimacy they shared was intoxicating. She couldn't think. Couldn't breathe without feeling him, scenting him. He encompassed her every inch and molecule.

Fire raged over her skin and inside her body as well. She felt consumed in the literal sense, as if he were taking her over. Conquering her. For a second she resisted, some final streak of independence insisting that she hold out. But it was stupid, and useless. James Waters had crept not only under her skin but into her heart. He owned her—body and soul.

For one moment she felt fear, but then El understood that this was what love was. Real love. Honest and lasting. It was handing herself over to someone without restrictions or strings. Buoyed by that understanding, she relinquished the last of her concerns and doubts. El opened herself to this man, embraced everything he could give her.

The final small muscles within her relaxed and pleasure overrode everything else. She threw her head back, her hair falling down her spine and over her shoulders. She arched her back and thrust her hips, accepting everything James was.

As if he knew she'd finally turned herself over to him completely, James shouted and began to pound into her. His thrusts were harder, longer and filled her deeper. El stimulated her clit with a blurring speed, feeling that golden moment just shimmering on the horizon. Her lungs felt like they would burst with the need for more air, but she couldn't suck it in fast enough. Her whole body seized up, balanced precariously on the pinnacle of ultimate satisfaction.

James tilted his hips, bringing them closer together. And as he moved back within her, his cock grazed along her inner walls, rubbing over the myriad of nerves. El shrieked, hurled over the edge as her eyes squeezed instinctively shut. Her orgasm detonated within her body, shuddering as the waves of pleasure rolled over and through her. Her back bowed, as if an electrical current ran through her.

The scream she emitted sounded unlike anything she'd heard before. Starting low, then gathering in volume and intensity, it was an animalistic, raw cry of release and bliss.

James was only a pace behind her. Wanting to watch him come, El forced her eyes open and turned her head. Caught up in his ecstasy, James looked almost in pain. His back bowed, his hips thrust forward as he pounded into her, riding through his orgasm. His eyes were squeezed tightly shut and his mouth gaped as he roared his release.

Warmth suffused her anal passage as he filled her with seed. El could feel it hot and liquid as he emptied himself in her. Deliciously sore, filled with his essence, exhaustion washed over her. Arms and legs wobbled as their physical exertions took their toll.

"Let me help you, baby. Bloody hell that was...beyond description," James murmured softly to her. He wrapped his arm around her waist and helped her down as she lowered her body to the luscious embrace of the bed. He followed her down and spooned her, holding their bodies close together.

El closed her eyes, overwhelmed but happier and more sated than she had ever been in her life. Her arse ached and she could feel that pleasant tug of pain in many of her muscles — rather like she felt after a good, hard workout at the gym. Shifting her legs to partly turn, she felt the twinge in her upper thighs, her lower back and a few other more sensitive places — places the gym didn't work out.

She pressed a kiss to James' jaw, love filling her up.

"That was amazing," she said softly. "Thank you."

"As I said earlier, it was every inch of my pleasure," he returned in a low tone. El wrapped her arm lightly around his waist, snuggled into the comfort of his embrace and closed her eyes.

In this golden, glowing moment she felt life was perfect and couldn't possibly ever get better than this.

* * * *

Ravenous, El sat on the couch, picked up a half of the enormous sandwich James had made earlier and took a huge bite out of it. Tastes exploded over her tongue, filling her mouth and making it water. She couldn't remember the last time she'd enjoyed a meal more. Silence reigned between them as she and James sat comfortably close on the couch, devouring the food.

Still damp from the shower they'd both taken, El felt refreshed and re-energized. She knew when she had a full stomach she'd be able to hit the case with a new vigor. James had been right. She could be cranky and short-tempered when hungry. She all but inhaled the first half of her sandwich. Picking up the other half, she let herself relax, no longer starving. Taking a slower bite, she then consciously chewed it more thoughtfully, enjoying the mix of flavors and the act of sharing a meal with her lover.

"Does it bother you to be working both sides of the fence this time?" El asked after she'd swallowed. James shot her a perplexed look, his mouth full. She chuckled and explained. "We're looking for a stolen painting, hoping to outsmart the bad guys and unravel the intricate web they've laid out. Hell, if we get really lucky, we can even poke out an explanation as to why this particular painting is so important and even understand who else wants it and stop them. Usually you're on the other end, plotting to avoid the cops — or whoever — and outsmart the security systems and match wits with the supposed experts."

"You know it's not usually that black and white," James chided.

El nodded, completely accepting his point.

"Absolutely. I've recently seen first-hand how manipulative and easily tempted the supposed good guys can be and turn to their own selfish need and profit. I'm not poking you here. Often people turn to stealing or working against the establishment not for greed or personal gain, but to right wrongs when their hands are otherwise tied. That wasn't my point — it was you're completely on the other end here. You aren't breaking in or trying to get into a system, you're trying to recover something already stolen, trace back the steps and piece together what happened after it was taken. It surely is a different perspective for you."

"In some ways, sure." James shrugged and took another bite of food. After he'd swallowed he continued, "I'm not sure I've told you, but recently I've expanded my horizons into consulting. I did a lot of soul searching once I realized you weren't necessarily coming back. I've only dabbled in smaller projects for a few years now, taken what I consider jobs that have more...altruistic or perhaps noble causes. That was already changing before we even met. You've had a profound effect on me, whether you realize it or not, Eleanor. I've been helping people who need to break systems and learn how to unwind those knots and webs you just described."

El dropped her jaw open. She scanned James' face, trying to see if he was pulling her leg or just trying to bamboozle her. He seemed serious.

"You're helping others crack systems? To steal? You're...what, training them? James... You can't possibly control what they do with that knowledge. I've always understood you're an inherently good man—you'd never go in somewhere, guns blazing, and kill innocents, or rob people who couldn't afford it or be...well, nasty like that. But if you're training others, that's out of your control. I don't understand."

"People can use that knowledge for good," James insisted calmly. He seemed unfazed by her concern. "Take your own co-workers, for example. I'm sure you have some remarkably talented people, but you surely have more cases than experts. Neither you nor Robert know how to hack—how do you approach your work when that is called for?"

"That's completely different," she protested. "We have consultants, experts who are suitably aware of the importance of the work we do and know our need for secrecy. We rarely give them all the pertinent details, but explain the system we need to hack or the type of problem we're facing and they help us without needing to know every detail of the case itself. They're separate, but well used contacts the Agency has—Oh."

El paused mid-tirade. James' eyes were filled with laughter, the grin spreading across his face as he struggled to contain it. Her brain put the pieces together quickly. She widened her eyes in surprise.

"You're kidding me?" she choked out. "You've become a consultant? For us? That's... Well, not impossible, obviously. But how can I have not run across you in the office or during briefings? How long have you been doing this? What level clearance do you have?"

Her hunger forgotten, she placed the partly eaten food onto the plate and peppered him eagerly with questions, her curiosity brimming over. James continued to eat, a smug look in his eyes. He kept silent, a smile hovering. In that moment he appeared as secretive as a naughty schoolboy.

"So much for your bad boy appeal," she finished, teasing him.

"Don't get too excited, darling," he said after swallowing the last of his meal. "Trust me, you haven't reformed me. Not by a long shot. I've kept my hand in. I look at this as broadening my horizons. I get to charge an outrageous amount to prove where the holes are in various systems. Every now and then I even get to go out into the field and crack them. Much as it shames me to admit it, I've enjoyed a few very robust arguments with other contractors and have proven my point by showing them exactly what I mean in person. I'm still dabbling and freelancing once in a while too—though I'd appreciate if you didn't spread that far and wide. I'm straddling the line between respectable and disreputable quite well, even if I do say so myself."

El shifted, kneeling up on the couch, then straddled James, settling comfortably in his lap. Resting her hands lightly on his shoulders, she then kissed him with a brief, chaste press of lips. She enjoyed tasting the pickles from his meal along with the other flavors beneath.

"I find the thought of you still being a bit naughty, not completely turned to the side of good, yet still working with us and dabbling on the side, extremely appealing," she said with brutal honesty. "It's rather hot, thinking of you working for us, but still with the stealthy thief lurking underneath. It's like a delicious secret we share between us and don't let anyone else in on."

James grinned. "Well now, it's not a *secret* secret, but far be it for me to dampen anything that makes you hot. We can share telling glances when we're in the same briefing. That could prove fun as well as distracting."

El kissed him, pulling away only as he dipped his hands into the waistband of her pants and cupped her arse.

"I'm really motivated now," she said. "Let's go back to the start, go over the basics. Bet you anything we find a few points we've missed earlier. "

James stared at her. It took her a moment to realize why he looked perplexed. She'd managed to switch gears and barely blink. It took him a minute longer to catch up. Leaning forward, she got her balance, then pressed a hot kiss against his lips and tried to smother her laugh.

"Adrenaline surge," she explained. "Right now I'd love nothing more than to fuck you blind right here, but we've got work to do."

El swung a leg around, lifted herself up and settled next to him on the couch. With quick fingers she booted up the laptop again, pulling up the files from the network.

"Does your printer have Wi-Fi?" she asked, not even looking up from the screen. James rose and crossed to where a small desk sat in the far corner of the room. Glancing quickly, she saw him switch a printer on, the small green light blinking as it warmed up.

Her mind was busy. She clicked on the icon and started selecting files to load onto the printer, so she could share the load with James. Trusting him fully, she printed everything she and Rob had been given and collected themselves on the case.

Chapter Seven

El sipped at her mug of tea, her brain whirling as she re-accumulated all the data. As usually happened with the cases, some data was old, some updated and a few interim reports had been submitted over the last few hours. Everything was uploaded onto the network to be easily accessed by everyone working the case.

While some of the finer details were still sketchy — laboratory tests often took hours or even days to come to fruition — she believed that every piece helped show more of the larger picture. Revisiting the caseload as a whole was always a good idea. Things that didn't appear connected when viewed by themselves often could snap together when reviewed as a whole, one after the other.

Carefully lowering her mug to the coaster James had provided, El then picked up a highlighter and flicked through the report on Luke's flat. Realizing there was only one page to the report, she turned the sheet of paper over, then checked on the laptop that there wasn't more that she'd missed.

No dice.

The report of the search of Luke's flat only had one page to it. Almost nothing at all had been found. No laptop, no diagrams, no plans, no schematics of the Gallery. Nada.

"That can't be right," El murmured to herself. Her instincts stirred, insisted there would be some evidence of the heist. Months of planning didn't just vaporize without a trace.

Intrigued, she scrounged through some papers until she found the sheet that listed the items Luke had been taken into custody with—wallet, keys, phone, a few pounds worth of coins, a couple of euros, a memory stick. El snapped to attention, stopping at the USB.

"What are the chances you'd have a data storage device, say a USB, on your person if you didn't have a laptop or some means of reading it? A laptop, or computer somewhere?" she asked, turning to James.

He lifted his head, blinked his eyes as he thought for a moment.

"It's possible, but not very logical. Why?"

"The search of Luke's apartment, a lot of the lab analysis—hair, fibers and the like—isn't in, but the physical inventory is practically empty. No laptop, desktop, plans, there's nothing useful found."

"Maybe he had everything stashed elsewhere?"

"I don't think so." El shook her head and pulled out another sheet of paper, handing it to James. "Look, the warehouse had some stuff, but Chelsea and David explained that had been cleaned out. There's no sense to Luke having two residences here. Between the warehouse and his flat, that was plenty for him. So where is the evidence that will lock him away?"

"I thought we had him solid on multiple charges?"

"Oh we do. That's not what I'm getting at. His flat should have had *some* evidence. Discarded plans of attack, security logs, notes. Hell, who nowadays doesn't have a laptop or computer of some form and Internet connections? It's almost unheard of. We've missed something at his flat. The search was too fast, or the agents were tired and not thinking straight."

"You want to go back there," James stated.

"I'd appreciate your take on it all," she agreed sweetly. "Just think of how wonderful it will feel to charge overtime for a simple look around the place. Besides, I bet you can offer some genuine insight."

"You mean I won't be completely ripping off the Agency?" he teased.

She laughed and stood. "I'll cook you dinner one night this week. Your choice of meal. Think of it as incentive."

"Mmm, you make me feel like I've been charging the wrong price for my services," James murmured as he wrapped an arm around her waist and drew her close. El clung to him, pressing snugly along the line of his chest, loving the fact that she could do so practically at whim now.

Anticipation rose as he lowered his head by degrees until finally she lost patience, closed the gap between them and kissed him passionately. Their lips fused together, the world melting away. El knew she'd never get tired of touching James, tasting him, feeling him right then next to her every step of the way.

After a moment, they both pulled apart. El's heart pumped harder and her face flushed as she caught the molten look in James' eyes. The temptation to ignore her instincts, throw caution to the wind and ravish her lover here and now was strong. She pushed it down, reminding herself they had time — hopefully forever —

to spend together, taking one another and indulging every chance possible.

Right now, they had a job to do.

Sighing with regret, she pulled out of his embrace.

"We need to move," she said. James sucked in a deep breath, seemed to calm himself then nodded.

"I'll grab my stuff. Let's go."

* * * *

"Is it bad that a part of me wants to offer to let you pick the lock?" El said as she twisted the key in Luke's lock. She threw James a laughing look over her shoulder as she opened the door.

They'd swung by HQ to collect Calloway's keys and sign the chain of custody form. El had hoped that they'd run into Robert, but he'd gone when they arrived. The thought of calling him again had crossed her mind, but they'd been working since very early in the morning and if Rob had decided he needed some sleep or downtime, El was reluctant to disturb that.

"Keeping my skills fresh is never a bad idea," James replied. "But this is a standard door lock. Not only could I crack it in my sleep, but should I decide I needed the practice, I could do it on my own flat and not attract nearly so much attention."

El chuckled as James closed the door behind them. She wandered around the neat, almost sparse flat to try to get her mind back into the game. She enjoyed working with James, teasing him and sharing this side of herself with him, but in so many ways he was a distraction Rob just wasn't. El enjoyed it, but knew she couldn't have James as her full-time partner. Her efficiency would fall through the floor, not to mention that chances were good she'd miss critical steps because she'd be caught up in the way that tight arse of his moved in his pants, or she'd get a head full of naughty fantasies from a casual smile he threw her way.

It was a quick way to get herself killed, and she had every intention of living a long, full life with this man.

A circuit around the flat didn't show El much at all. Powder smudges and that slightly ruffled look overall showed a crew had already been through, but still the entire area felt temporary. This clearly wasn't a home, but more of a transition, somewhere to sleep, eat, wash and get out of.

While James continued looking — El noticed he was careful to not touch any surface — she stood in the small bedroom, turned a slow circle and tried to figure out what she was missing. After she completed the glance around the room, she repeated it in the opposite direction.

This would be the space Luke felt most comfortable in, safest. It was instinct to rest, relax and sleep with the feeling of security. Most often people would hide things in the privacy of their bedroom, whether it be jewelry, money, dirty books or toys, whatever. It was human nature to use one's private space to stash these sorts of things.

Something gnawed at the edge of her consciousness. El tapped a foot in a fast, snapping manner, trying to figure out what it was. Frustrated — feeling like she had a word right on the tip of her tongue but couldn't place it — she searched the room herself.

She ran through all the obvious places — under the bed, beneath the drawers of the bedside table, under the alarm clock and in the back of the drawers. She opened the built-in wardrobe as James entered the room.

"Something's off here," she insisted. "I can feel it, I just can't place it. This is going to drive me mental if I don't work it out soon."

As she pushed through the two dozen coat hangers one by one, she studied the three pairs of shoes lined up neatly on the floor. Sighing, she decided she'd need to feel the linings of the jackets, then the trousers. Not that Calloway could hide a laptop there, but maybe a key card, or some form of key. Hell, right now she'd take a scrap of paper with a fortune cookie with a philosophical riddle written on it.

"Well, that closet is off for starters," James remarked.

El froze, looked around the inside of the closet. "What do you mean? I don't see anything strange about it."

"Look," James explained patiently. He came up beside her, reached out his arm and roughly measured the depth of the closet. Leading her through the doorway into the adjacent bathroom, he then pointed out the shared wall.

"It's shallow," he admitted, "but there's definitely some lost space here. This bathroom would definitely be deeper along that wall. Maybe half a foot or more."

"A safe of some sort," El said excitedly. "Or even just a hidey-hole. That's fantastic. Perfect. Let's hope Luke has a stash— Oh, fuck me blind, what if we've been over-thinking this all along? They had less than two hours to hide the painting. What if Luke didn't trust anyone? If I had a secret safe, somewhere I knew no one else could find my stuff, sure I'd place a priceless painting there after I'd stolen it."

Almost bouncing on the balls of her feet, she raced back to the bedroom and into the cupboard. James was only a pace behind her.

"It has to be here," she insisted. "That makes so much sense. It's the only answer that fits."

Tapping the wall, she soon found a panel right in the middle just above eye level that was loose.

"Hang on," James stepped up to her, exerting gentle pressure on her shoulder to push her back. "Let's not rush in too blindly."

Barely suppressing her impatience, El lifted up onto her toes and peered over James' shoulder as he tapped around the panel before he pressed his face against the wall and squinted.

"No use, I can't see behind the crack in the wood," he muttered.

El desperately wanted to growl at him to just open it, *damn it*, but she had to concede that this was James' field of expertise. She wouldn't take kindly to him telling her how to organize a bust or run an interview. He didn't need her to tell him how to crack a secret hidey-hole.

"Better hope there isn't a fail-safe on this baby," James said without even glancing back at her.

El blinked, her brain taking a second or two to register what he was saying. Surely he didn't mean... "Wait, if you think we might be about to blow this place up — ?"

"Ten seconds ago you were all but breathing fire at me, darling." James smirked.

El opened her mouth silently, not sure where to even start with that. Before she could summon the common sense to urge caution, he removed the panel.

She squeezed her eyes shut, half expecting an explosion or blast of fire to stream out.

Nothing.

She huffed out a sigh, torn between annoyance and laughter.

"Well shit," James cursed. El peered over his shoulder and gulped.

They'd exposed a keypad and thick steel door. El would have been thrilled had there not been a small square of soft gray-colored plastique adhered to the door and linked by numerous wires to a small digital display.

5:00 turned to 4:59 to 4:58.

El's heart damn near stopped.

"Holy shit," she cursed as she whipped out her phone.

"Don't bother," James said calmly, working his dexterous fingers nimbly at the keypad already. He withdrew a small console the size of a paperback book from the pocket of his leather jacket. Two thin electrodes snapped into the box and attached to either side of the keypad.

El watched, entranced—she refused to think of it as frozen—as James began typing a sequence of dizzying numbers with a blurring speed.

Not wanting to distract James, she thought for a moment about why she shouldn't make any calls. With such a short period of time given to them, she decided it would be redundant. No way could anyone else arrive before the place blew up. Besides, mobile phones were ignition points, and El didn't have a clue if making a call could set off the charge prematurely.

The amount of plastique looked small. Large enough to make this flat a smoking crater, she presumed, when the timer finished, but not enough to take out much collateral damage.

4:31, 4:30, 4:29.

El took a deep breath and returned her phone to her pocket. Beads of sweat ran down her spine. She calmed her breathing and emptied her mind. No use getting her knickers into a twist.

"The blast will destroy whatever's in the safe, won't it?" she said, pleased but shocked at how steady her voice sounded.

"I think that's the intent. If Calloway wanted to blow half of London up, this isn't how he'd do it. I figure it's just a fail-safe. It's a crude but formidable deterrent to anyone if they tried to pry into what wasn't their business."

"The Cezanne better be in here," she muttered.

"Bloody hell, yes. You know, darling, you could wait outside. Three minutes is plenty of time for you to get that luscious arse to safety."

El crossed her arms over her chest and frowned.

"I'll pretend you didn't just say that. Not only am I not leaving you here like some skanky whore, but this is my operation. It's my responsibility to get the painting, not yours. You can always—"

"Don't even suggest it. Neither of us want you to finish that sentence," he growled. "Damned if I'm going to let a slippery amateur like Calloway beat me like this. Come on, you bitch, finish that sequence."

El understood that he spoke to either the console or the keypad, not her. She grinned and tried not to focus on the digital timer.

3:17, 3:16, 3:15.

A bead of sweat slid down from James' temple.

"I love you," she blurted out. Embarrassed, she blushed and pressed her lips together. James cast her a second-long glance, his brow furrowed.

"Don't joke about that. Not now, please."

"I'm not kidding. I realized it earlier, while you were reaming my arse, actually, but I didn't want to say it. I thought it might scare you, or you'd think it was the sex talking, not my heart. But I'm serious. I'm not a child, I know how I feel. And I love you. Adore you silly."

James cursed a streak and shot her another look. He seemed exasperated, elated and frustrated.

"I love you to the point of insanity, which you've nearly pushed me to just now. Of all the bloody times to... I love you, El. Madly. Truly. Completely."

El grinned, feeling bizarrely smug considering the circumstances. She didn't need to look at the timer anymore. Instead, she rested her palm lightly at the base of James' spine, happy to just have the small but intimate contact with him.

"Almost, almost, almost there," he chanted under his breath. A digital beep sounded and for a single, heart-stopping moment she thought the plastique was about to detonate. A metallic click filled the air and she watched James swing open the safe's door. El twisted her head to check the timer.

1:07... The numbers were frozen—stopped by the keypad being unlocked and thus deactivated.

She heaved an enormous sigh of relief.

James cupped her jaw and tilted her face up to his. They kissed slowly, tenderly. The passion was still present between them, but this was a relieved kiss of simple, sweet elegance.

"Too late to take those words back," he murmured as they separated by an inch or two.

El chuckled. "I have no desire to take anything back. I might have preferred to wait a little, but more time isn't going to alter how I feel for you. I love you, James Waters. With all my heart."

"And I you," he replied. They kissed again briefly, then James stepped away. He waved an arm at the open safe and indicated that she should have first look.

"Thank you," she said with a smile, then eagerly peered into the shallow recess.

Three shelves were almost empty. A laptop sat in a corner with a few neatly bundled stacks of hundred pound notes. Most excitingly of all, a cardboard tube was propped in the corner, looking innocuous and innocent. El had to restrain herself from clapping her hands in glee like a child surveying an unexpected present.

"Oh boy, I really hope this is what I want it to be," she cheered.

El turned to James, but didn't need to ask. He already held out a pair of latex gloves. She slipped them on like a pro and picked up the tube. Popping the lid off, she then took a slow, deep breath. She couldn't help but dance a little in place as she saw a rolled up piece of canvas.

Removing it reverently, with as much care as she could muster, El stepped toward the bed. She dropped the cardboard tube to the floor and unrolled the painting, spreading it out over the duvet so they could both examine the work.

The painting was created from bold colors. The entire canvas was filled with the hilly landscape of a park or perhaps a forest. Trees lined the edge of the canvas, with a dark or twilight shade of night filling the sky. A walking path cut north to south right in the center of the image. The background was predominantly in greens and browns. Couples on either side sat or lay together on the grass, but they were hazy, muted almost, and scattered across small nooks. Swiftly, El counted eight in total, but even to her untrained eye it was clear that these couples were just incidentals in the background.

Front and center were the main couple. Cezanne had drawn in clear, great detail, a gorgeous man and woman. A blonde Caucasian woman was clasped in the embrace of an olive-skinned, dark-haired man. They were both stunningly naked.

El didn't know if it was her own current frame of mind, or perhaps the edgy darkness of the canvas itself, but the embrace seemed intimate, passionate and possibly even forced. The nakedness of the couple along with the fact that the woman's body was arched, the man clasping her to him, reminded her of how in the heat of sensual lovemaking, anyone could look as though they were in ecstasy or pain.

Now she looked further, she wondered if, in fact, this mid-climax was what Cezanne had captured. While at first she had thought the man might be forcing the woman, it could just as easily be that they were clenched together, locked mid-coitus. Whichever it was, the man and woman had eyes and senses fully riveted only upon each other. Forced or consensual, the painting reeked of intimacy, sensuality and the burning intensity only the greatly aroused and highly inflamed erotic senses can be.

"It's a powerful piece, isn't it?" she murmured.

James peered at it over her shoulder. "Powerful, enticing, erotic and faintly disturbing," he agreed, his gaze roaming over the canvas.

El had the feeling that James could look for years at this piece and never grow tired of it. She thought he tried to consume it with his eyes alone. Returning her own gaze, she understood. The piece was compelling to say the least. She wouldn't mind a copy of it herself, a cheap print she could place somewhere that would catch her eye frequently. Enticing and clearly controversial, she understood how deeply elemental this image could prove to be, to many people, regardless of their artistic tastes.

"Art is frequently controversial," she commented. "I bet people have argued since this was first shown, about whether this is the intoxicating embrace of passionate love, or something darker, more despondent."

"I couldn't agree more. But then, that's why so often we close the door on our most private moments. Viewed from the outside and out of context, many things can appear completely different from what they are."

"Absolutely," she agreed, looking up at him. They shared a speaking glance. El felt her heart overflow with love.

"I've got to call this in, and I need to leave another message for Rob. James... Thank you. For everything."

James cupped her jaw and they shared a lingering, passionate kiss. El could sense a lifetime's worth of passion burning in the kiss and it made her heart sing. When they pulled away she had to restrain herself from dragging him close for more. Flying high on the thrill of success, she pulled out her phone again. James rolled the Cezanne back up and replaced it in the tube. El pressed the speed dial for Rob's phone.

Frowning as she got his voicemail again, she tried to shrug off her worry.

"Rob, it's El. We've found it! The...erm, painting." Only at the last minute did she recall the lack of privacy and safety of mobile phones. Discretion was always needed on these. "Look, I know you need a break, some sleep, but seriously— We've got it. James and I are heading back to HQ. There was a safe in the target's flat. It's complicated, but we've recovered what we need. Get back to me, soon."

"Should we swing by Robert's place?" James offered.

El thought about that for a moment then shook her head.

"I'll give him an hour to contact me. We'll send out the cavalry if I don't hear from him soon. I'm probably a little oversensitive since it's not every day I come face to face with a safe wrapped in explosives. I'm understandably twitchy and paranoid now. Besides, Calloway and the others are safely locked up. We're just wrapping up loose ends here."

James slung his arm around her shoulders and handed her the tube with the Cezanne safely stored within. She grinned, unable to hide her pleasure at both having possession of the painting and the man next to her.

"We did good," she complimented him. His gaze as it rested upon her face was filled with love.

"Too right, we did. Let's go brag to Waldron and the others."

Nodding, she let him guide her from the room, more than happy to follow where he led.

ICY CONTROL

Dedication

With love and thanks, as always — to my ladies, Lily, Billi and Sue. ☺

Chapter One

"Where's your partner, Stevens?"

Robert Stevens glanced up from his computer screen and swiveled around in his seat. Gary Waldron stood behind him, his back military-straight as he glanced at the currently empty desk of Rob's colleague and work-partner, Eleanor Williams. Rob scratched at his jaw and hid the grin that wanted to peep out.

While Waldron was a good boss, matchmaking on the Agency's time was not something he would have condoned. Far from being a fool, Rob knew that nudging El toward the man who held her heart was playing with fire — both with his friendship with El and by wasting the Agency's time. He knew he shouldn't have indulged, but El had been miserable without James.

Rob's friendship with the fiery redhead was deep and strong. He and El were excellent partners and Rob doubted the not-so-subtle setting up job he'd done would have been taken with such grace had anyone else laid it out for her. Still, Waldron didn't need to know the finer details, or not those that didn't relate to their current case.

"El's questioning an external source," Rob replied. As far as it went, it was truth, just not the *complete* story. "She has an associate who has ties to the legitimate and greyer sides to the art world."

"Still no sign of that damn Cezanne?" Waldron sighed.

Rob shook his head. "Not so far, sir. But it's hardly been twenty-four hours. Calloway, Brown and Phillipe are all in custody and not going anywhere. That means everyone directly responsible for the attack on the National Gallery and the heist of the painting are out of circulation and detained with us. Our chances of recovering the Cezanne are really good. El is following a lead with James Waters and I'm here scrounging for any and all alternate routes of inquiry we can chase."

Waldron huffed out a short laugh. "You sound like your damn report."

The words weren't sharp or annoyed, but the political weight coming from this case and the fallout from the attack on the Gallery was starting to wear on those involved.

"Give me something I can feed these vultures, Stevens. I have the Mayor on the line every hour and half, the damn aristocracy baying for the blood of those responsible for sullying the Gallery's good name and reputation. I've told them we have custody of those responsible, but without answers to why this happened and the restitution of the painting, it's going to get political and ugly very quickly."

Rob nodded. He ran a hand tiredly over his short, dark brown hair. He and El had been woken up around three that morning when the second attack on the Gallery had occurred and all hell had broken loose. He'd not had a break since. He was starting to feel every minute of his thirty-eight years. No longer could he work thirty or forty hours in a row without pause—as the gray sprinkling at his temples now started to warn him.

"We're on it, sir," Rob said, unsure what else he could say. "El and Waters are chasing things up. I'll call her for an update within the hour. I'm catching up on this morning's reports and can have a preliminary summary in your email before the lunch hour is over if you wish."

"Sometime before my three p.m. meeting is adequate," Waldron conceded with a sigh. "I'd prefer to have some nugget to give them rather than a load of double-talk that means nothing. You and Williams are the best, though. Do us proud and prove it once more."

Rob agreed silently. Waldron took a step then paused. His brow furrowed as he seemed to try to recall something, then turned to face Rob again. He had no idea why, but Rob braced himself as if for a verbal punch. Waldron didn't disappoint, proving Rob's instincts were as honed as ever.

"Didn't you have a school chum who was a semi-professional artist? A pretty dark-haired girl. I recall my missus dragged me to a showing of hers for our anniversary a year ago and we bumped into each other there. What was her name?"

"Sally." Rob cleared his throat when his voice cracked slightly. He didn't need to think about which friend it had been—El was already on his case to go and chat to his oldest, closest friend. "Sally Langtry."

"Langtry, that's right." Waldron nodded.

He narrowed his eyes at Rob, searching his face. Rob maintained his bland, innocent expression. "Have you contacted her? Or is there a good reason not to? We need to pull out all the stops here. You understand that, right?"

"Of course. I'm keeping abreast of the information we have and then will contact Sally soon. She works late most nights and has another showing in a few weeks, so it would be rude to call her much before noon."

Waldron took a telling and slow glance at his watch. "I'll expect you to call her any minute now, as it's almost half an hour past noon. By the way, my wife adores Miss Langtry's work. When you have a date for her upcoming showing, I'd appreciate you giving me a heads up. I can curry some favor by getting tickets before Linda has to badger me for them."

Rob grinned, appreciating Waldron lightening the mood and softening the order to at least outwardly appear more of a request than the command it truthfully was.

"Absolutely, sir."

"Thank you." Waldron clasped Rob's shoulder in a friendly manner. With a quick nod Waldron continued toward his office.

Rob sighed when his boss was out of earshot.

Rob rubbed his face. The last thing he'd wanted was to bring this to Sal's door. She had always been soft, innocent and eccentric. He'd been half in love with his high school friend since they were teenagers. Rob knew this was the main reason El had teased, poked and hassled him to consult with his whimsical friend. El was a firecracker, a damn fine detective and intense in most areas of her life. The very fact she'd not been subtle in her attempt to set him up and force him into to consulting Sally proved how strongly El felt that they'd be right together. Rob wondered whether he'd really detached his feelings so much that he'd convinced himself there was really no hope for him and the gentle artist.

El just wanted him happy. He appreciated the gesture, but he was loath to bring violence, anger and darkness to Sal's door. There was something so pure and happy about her that he would've killed anyone who took that away from her. Sal was the eternal optimist and that was one of the main things he loved about her, the inherent goodness in her heart that went all the way to her core.

Asking her to look into the seedier side of the art world, to ask questions and search out the darker aspects he so frequently shouldered, wasn't something he wanted to do. But both El and Waldron had their points. People naturally confided in and spoke to Sally. She heard things many others never caught wind of.

Rob tapped his fingers against his desk, weighing his options.

Part of him longed to see her—it had been almost a month since they'd caught up over lunch—and he knew she'd not turn him away. More and more over the last year or so he'd felt chafed at the distance he kept between himself and Sally. He wanted her cheeky grin to be the last thing he saw at night before he closed his eyes. And wake up to her in the golden light of the morning.

Sal wouldn't make him go or refuse to offer every assistance, should he ask. He knew she'd not do that to anyone, should she think they needed help. It irked him how a few people used her in that way, taking from her emotionally when she was busy or tired. But that was a part of who she inherently was. Hospitality was a way of life for Sal, not just words or vague promises never kept.

"You're being stupid," he chided himself.

Sally was his friend. If she was busy, he could think of an excuse for Waldron and leave her be. Two small parts of Rob's brain fought—one insisting this was a perfect opportunity to catch up with Sal, the other warning him not to drag her into the shadows of his world.

"Now you're really pushing the envelope," he muttered. "Next thing you know you'll be failing the annual psych exam and they'll be carting you off. Just call the woman."

Rob picked up the phone. He began dialing but then stopped.

There was a small, privately owned bakery between the office and Sal's that made a fresh chive bread she adored. He could pick some up for her and surprise her with it. He knew she'd love that and he wanted to see the grin it would bring to her face. If he called her he'd talk her—or himself—out of the visit. And really, he *did* need her help.

Decided, he shuffled the reports into his leather-bound folder. Rob moved swiftly and refused to think. He switched his computer off and checked he had everything he'd need. Before he could debate further with himself and really risk his sanity, he left the office.

* * * *

"Oh, Bobby, you're an angel, that's exactly what I need."

Rob grinned and held the still steaming loaf out to Sally. Deep inside he was pleased to see her sniff the fresh bread, her eyes closed with ecstasy. His heart gave a quickening *pitter patter* and he had to swallow to bring moisture back into his mouth.

She was the only person he allowed to call him Bobby—just as he was the only one allowed call her Sal. It was a small intimacy they'd shared for more than two decades now, though neither of them had ever acknowledged just how special it was.

"I figured it was the least I could do if I was going to turn up unannounced on your doorstep."

"You know good and well that you're welcome— announced or not—any time, day or night, Robert," she chided. Only the wicked, happy twinkle in those big, beautiful green eyes belied the severity of her words. Soft red lips parted as she gasped, seeming shocked. "My manners have fled after your thoughtful gift distracted me."

Sally cradled the loaf in one arm and held the door to her small loft open with the other. "Please, Bobby. Come in and have a cup of tea. You seem exhausted. Overworking like always, I assume? How is El? What's been happening out there in the real world?"

"I'm not overworking, and El is very well, thank you. I do have a confession to make, however. I've come with an ulterior motive, I'm afraid."

Rob cast her a mildly sheepish look as she led the way to where a small kitchenette had been set up. She turned on the kettle and pulled two mugs from the dish draining rack.

The loft was open and airy with enormous, high ceilings and two walls made of floor-to-ceiling windows. As an artist's studio, it was perfect with so much natural light and roomy atmosphere. As a place to live in, Rob worried it was less than ideal. Uncomfortably cold in winter and stuffy in summer, there was no ducted heating or real climate control to speak of.

Add in the temperamental electricity and a hot water supply far closer to lukewarm than 'hot', half of his visits were to be certain nothing had broken down. Numerous times over the last few years, Rob had taken a weekend or longer fighting with various pieces of equipment that had given up the ghost, and sometimes he spent hours with the landlord or on the phone giving a more masculine, forceful insistence to the utility companies to send someone around to fix things.

Sal, bless her, used her time and money on paints, canvasses and supplies. As long as she could climb the spiral staircase to the tiny bedroom and bathroom occupied and find a warm bed, and the sun rose the following morning for her to paint by, she had few other cares about her surroundings or circumstances. Rob had other ideas on what was classified as 'bare essentials'. He worried when her heating broke down, or when she spent days without electricity because the company said they'd 'fix it soon' and never bothered to turn up.

The miniscule kitchenette held a hotplate, a small fridge and a bench with a kettle and toaster. Sally could become lost in her work for hours, days at a time and frequently subsisted on eating take-out or merely toast. It also wasn't uncommon for Rob to arrive and whisk her away for a decent meal—after the natural light had gone, of course. Her passion for the art she created was genuine.

"You haven't read the papers yet?" Rob asked, searching around.

Three easels were stationed in separate spots around the room. Each held works at various stages of completion. One was still only light sketches that he couldn't make out, another was a rural landscape and the third looked like it would end up as a whimsical piece of children playing in the playground. Rob could tell this, as there was an iron swing set on what he thought might be a concrete block, but also brightly colored fairies and pixies mingled with the kids.

He recognized the front page of the newspaper sitting on the coffee table as almost a week old. A mug rested next to it. Considering there were three pieces on the go and numerous palettes, paintbrushes and murky beakers of water scattered about, he figured Sally hadn't been keeping abreast of current events.

Guilt gnawed at him.

Did he really need to drag his friend, this woman he felt so strongly for, into the darkness that pocketed his life? The kettle boiled, switched itself off. Sally bent her head as she carefully poured the steaming water into the mugs and let the teabags steep.

Rob drank in her dark-chocolate-colored hair, admiring the pixie-style haircut she'd worn for a number of months now. The sassy, sexy style undeniably suited her, he loved how it made her sparkling, huge green eyes that much more luminous against her pale, delicate English skin. She reminded him of an impish fairy, like the ones she frequently painted into her more light-hearted pieces. Next to his six-foot-four frame, she often looked like one too, despite the fact she was five foot six in her bare feet.

Tea made, Sally handed him a mug and met his gaze. She studied him for a moment before resting her hand lightly on his arm and leading him toward the tattered couch. It sat against one of the enormous windows and overlooked the postage-stamp-sized garden. They sat and she took a sip of her tea before speaking.

"Okay, Bobby. It must be something pretty horrid to have you so quiet and reflective. I also know there must be a way I can help you — aside from being your friend and listening — or else you'd have waited to drag me out to dinner and feed me like you usually do. Tell me about it."

Rob told himself again that Sally was a fully grown woman and perfectly capable of giving him some advice. That was as far as this needed to go. Taking a deep breath, he knew that her curiosity would be roused by now and she'd end up getting the story out of him one way or the other.

"A small group of people nearly decimated the front of the National Gallery and stole a painting. They're in custody — there were a pair of agents from Dublin who'd been working undercover to break this ring — but the thieves managed to ditch the painting before we got our hands on them. El and I have been brought in to mainly find the Cezanne, but also answer what it is about this particular piece that has everyone so adamant they possess it."

"Ah, I'd wondered where El was but hadn't wanted to pry when you just said she was fine."

Rob couldn't keep the smile off his face. Trust Sal to latch onto the one personal thing he'd said and restrain her curiosity about the rest. He drank some of his tea, trying to control his pride. Maybe it was just Sally knew him far too well. She'd know for a certainty now he'd started that he'd tell her everything he possibly could without breaking the strict Agency privacy guidelines.

She waited patiently, her green gaze resting on him. When Rob thought of his matchmaking skills between El and James, his smile turned smug.

"I might have talked El into coming with me to see James Waters." He grinned, unable to help himself. He was pleased by his success in forcing what he hoped would turn into a reconciliation between his partner and the man she so clearly loved. "She's been miserable without him these last few months and wasn't keen to face him again. But I pointed out few people know the art world like a semi-reformed thief, and she couldn't argue with that."

"And then you left her to it when you'd got her to his doorstep?" Sally chortled.

Rob nodded. "I might have discovered something far more pressing once we'd knocked on his door. They need time to get their feet under them again."

"I'm amazed. Not that you pulled it off, mind, but that she didn't try and perform a similar trick on us before you could do that."

"She tried," he admitted. "Practically her first thought was that you might have some information, or insight into rumors or maybe folklore or superstition surrounding the piece. We're drawing a big blank and pressure is mounting for answers."

"I hear all kinds of things. It's sorting out the stuff you should pay attention to from the gibberish you need to ignore that I struggle with. I'd feel terribly guilty if I set you off on a chase after a pot of gold that turned out to be brass."

Rob drank more of his tea. An easy silence fell between them. After a minute, he carefully placed his mug on the floor beside the couch where he wouldn't kick it accidently. He moved on the cushion then lifted a leg up to more comfortably face her.

"Art and painting is your passion, not just some passing hobby. You've studied the alchemy of it and practically every form it can take. It's no secret you're happily obsessed, and people respond to that and your inherent nature. They confide in you." Rob reached out and took her hands, turning them to show off the smears of paint and smaller stains she'd not been able to fully remove from the previous day. "You're an amazing woman and I'm not concerned if you send me off on a dozen dead ends. I can use all the help I can get."

"Well, heaven knows I owe you more favors than I could ever repay," Sally teased him, turning her hands in his to clasp him then squeezing lightly. "Don't think I've forgotten all I owe you, going right back to tenth form when I followed you down behind the sheds and found you smoking with a bunch of the boys. I was so keen to impress you, I beat you to it the following day and nearly coughed up a lung for my troubles. Not only did you quit immediately but gave me such a scolding I've not picked up a smoke since."

"Neither have I." Rob laughed, recalling the time well.

He'd seen Sally there, far shorter, only half grown and appearing so delicate amongst the rough crowd he'd hung out with in those days. She'd been determinedly puffing away, her eyes shining brightly with mingled fear and excitement to be in with the 'cool' guys. The others had leered at her, teasing her despite the fact she clearly wasn't used to smoking and didn't enjoy it in the least. It was the first time he'd felt the hot surge of protectiveness for her and he'd gotten into a fight with his so-called friends when he'd tried to ferry her away.

Rob also recalled later that year they'd shared a few sweet, stolen kisses. Glancing at her red lips, he wondered if she still tasted the same.

Sally smiled and her soft mouth parted. "Do you know which painting was stolen?" she asked after a moment. "Or have a copy of it for me to look at? I'll help you however I can, Bobby, you know that."

"Oh, right," he mumbled, still distracted by her mouth. He scooted to the edge of the couch, unzipped his leather folder and thumbed through the mound of papers until he came to a blurry but legible copy of the painting he'd downloaded earlier from the Gallery's website.

Sally took a final sip of her tea then placed the mug on the table before taking the paper from him.

"Oh, oh yes, I know this piece," she murmured, devouring the picture hungrily with her eyes.

Even upside down, Rob could see the appeal of the painting. With strong, bold strokes the artist had created a vivid piece. Dark blues and greens showed what Rob took to be a night-time scene in a park or forest, the garden and trees in the vicinity heavily shadowed. Indistinct couples were scattered here and there, part of the background and clearly unimportant to its creator.

Front and center was a naked couple, locked together in a desperate, passionate embrace. The woman reared back as if in ecstasy — or pain — her pale skin luminous, almost glowing. Her long blonde hair flowed as if in a breeze. Clasping her was an olive-skinned, dark-haired man. Their embrace was volatile, intimate. Rob had the distinct impression both the man and woman were on the verge of losing control — for right or wrong.

It made him nervous and excited simultaneously.

Wanting her reaction untainted by his own thoughts and questions, he waited as Sally looked her fill. It was impossible to tell, in his opinion, whether the scene was one of devout lovemaking or something much darker. This could be a passionate, stolen moment between a pair of lovers, or a dark moment. The heavier colors could easily indicate something not meant to be viewed, a scene of a woman being raped in the most brutal and desperate of ways.

It was all in the eye of the beholder.

"It's strongly painted," Sally said without lifting her gaze from the piece of paper. "It's bold. I'd think he wanted people to stare at it and whisper in awe, discuss the meanings and ramifications of his work.

"This isn't meant to be a sweet picture, made for the dining room or a lady's parlor. I mean look at it. This isn't a romantic portrait or perfectly executed bowl of fruit. This is meant to inspire passion and arguments. People would debate about the meaning and hold strong opinions on it. I bet if you showed it to a dozen people, some would be outraged, others offended and perhaps even a few titillated. And the arguments about whether it's a passionate lover's clench or something murkier, depraved, would keep people interested for hours. It's meant to garner a response not leave the viewer unmoved. I think the fact they're both in the grip of strong passion, on the edge of desire—or perhaps about to lose control of themselves—is clear for anyone to see.

"But even that is subjective," Sally remained focused on the paper. "This is an intense piece, yes, but all paintings that arouse strong feelings are. Something sexual and unfulfilled like this is always going to raise debate and conversation. I can easily think of a dozen different interpretations of this man and woman, and if I put my mind to it, I could probably triple that number with more esoteric or philosophical questions."

"Such as?" Rob found himself genuinely curious.

Sally placed the paper on the table and picked up her mug of tea. "Oh," she said with a rueful smile. "Any number of things. One of the easier discussions would be on how this could be a classic symbolism of the eternal power struggle between man and woman. Who ultimately is in control? The man who can use his physical strength? The woman and her sexual wiles? The one with greater intelligence? Or stubbornness? Or how about the one who loves the other more? And that's a simple way of looking at it."

Rob nodded, understanding her point and seeing there was far more beneath the surface than he'd even first assumed. He picked up his mug and finished his cooling tea. After placing the empty cup on the coffee table, he turned to fully face Sally again.

"But there has to be more than just vibrant discussion to this piece," he insisted. "People have been willing to kill over it. The front of the National Gallery is in ruins because these men wanted it so badly. They didn't go to all this trouble because they wanted to have possession of the piece for a critical discussion."

"Well, I have heard odd things about this painting, certainly. But nothing I'd care to write in a report for your superiors, Bobby. I already have a reputation for being strangely eccentric."

Rob reached out his hand, took Sal's and lightly squeezed her fingers. "We can start in confidence, Sal. I'll let you know if I need to use something. It's just us here."

"Always the charmer, aren't you, Bobby? Very well. Ever since the Gallery started showing it, I've heard all sorts of outlandish tales. Everything from the unbelievable to the mundane. One of the rumors I heard was that the elixir of life has been described within the number of strokes—that's always a kook's favorite fall back rumor. I've also heard there's a Rosetta stone style secret code key. I dismissed that story because there's no hint as to what it unlocks or how to decrypt the key itself. Personally, I'm of the opinion people want these sorts of items—paintings or otherwise—because it's there and they can take it."

"The greed of owning because you can." Rob nodded. He'd met many people like that in his time with the Agency. "Do you put any faith at all in these stories you've heard about?"

Sal studied him silently for a minute, her eyes seeming large in her petite face.

"Some of my friends who are more...shall we say, on the fringes of respectability, like to endlessly quote Horatio when these kinds of stories crop up around something. There are more things in Heaven and Earth... You know a part of me truly believes that. If you search deeply enough into something ordinary or commonplace, there can always be meanings hidden within meanings. If we take that to an extreme level say, you can believe quite honestly that something such as a leaf falling in your path is the world telling you to do something. Or if you're out for a drive and a shaft of sunlight falls on the road turning to your right, then that's the way you're *meant* to go."

"We've both always believed in fate, destiny."

"Yes, and we both have leanings toward believing in conspiracy theories." Sally grinned. "We're both prone to get carried away after a bottle of wine. In the past we've had some amazing, convoluted conversations that border on the paranoid. Anyone overhearing us would think we're extreme nutcases."

Rob laughed, knowing this and enjoying how they could discuss such things freely between themselves. Their long-standing friendship and the spark of what could potentially be between them spurred them both on to always one-up each other in those situations, and the addition of some wine and the cozy intimacy between them didn't hurt, either.

Sally got a faintly sad look to her. Rob sobered, about to ask what she'd thought of, but she beat him to the punch.

"I've never really understood, Bobby, how you could know some of the stranger aspects to my personality and not think I'm weird. Is it because we've known each other since our teens?"

He was surprised, unsure where this had sprung from.

"No, not at all. Sal, you're a fantastic woman, and I admire you greatly. We're both a little different. Neither of us think in what passes for 'normal', linear ways. But that's what makes us both so successful, don't you think? I enjoy the whimsy in so many of your paintings, at how you can find something we all take for granted and then add some magic, life and wonder into it. That's a talent so few people can lay claim to. I'm positive it's a big part of why so many people love your work."

"And your work?" she prodded. Her eyes sparkled.

Rob knew her well enough to know it wasn't from pleasure at his compliments, though she accepted them graciously. He knew if he brushed her prompting off, she'd wax lyrical. Saving her the trouble, he replied.

"Looking at things from a different perspective often means I piece the puzzle together to create an alternate picture. I might catch something others would overlook or take for granted, or see a glimmer of non-rational thought. It's often small things like this that start the knot of a problem unraveling. I'll certainly never be as popular as you, but El and I certainly have a reputation within the Agency. My boss' wife, by the way, is a huge fan of yours. I've been requested to give Waldron a heads up when your next showing will be."

"Nice try, Stevens," Sally teased him, lightly tapping his shoulder. "Changing the subject even as smoothly as you managed won't alter my mind or sway me in any way. But just so you won't get into trouble with your boss, my showing will be in about six to eight weeks, depending on how quickly I can finish up these last few pieces. I'll try and let you know as soon as I've confirmed the dates. Back to you, though, and our strange way of looking at the world."

"It's not strange, as such," he protested. "You certainly have nothing to be ashamed of. Anyone who says a derogative thing to you, I'll have strong words with. You're perfect in every way and I'll gladly break the bones of anyone who makes you feel otherwise."

The thought of Sal hurt, doubting or questioning herself made every protective instinct roar within him. Tired as he was, he didn't think to mask or soften the intensity of his passionate feelings. Only as Sal gasped did he realize he might have unwittingly shown too much. Quickly, he forced himself to calm down, to suppress the love that burned inside his heart and had for so long.

"No," she insisted vehemently and grabbed his hand again. "Bobby, for once lose that rigid control you have over yourself. How long have you been hiding that from me?"

Rob forced himself to catch her gaze and it stole his breath. Her eyes blazed with green fire. For a moment he thought he was dreaming, or imagining the depth of feeling raging within her. She shifted closer to him, her hand resting on his shoulder as she leaned into his body.

"The truth, Bobby. I won't shatter. I'm just not brave enough to admit it first," she insisted in a soft whisper.

It was as if she couldn't believe it, but for the first time ever, Rob was positive she *wanted* to believe he felt so passionately about her.

Rob tried to read more in her eyes, but now he doubted himself. He could swear he saw love and longing in her searing gaze. But still a part of him feared exposure and ruining the comfort and familiarity that had been between them for so long. He knew should he come clean and she didn't return the depths of his emotions, it would alter their friendship, the companionable way they were together. Should that happen, he'd never fully recover.

"Bobby," she whispered.

A frown appeared and he could feel uncertainty radiate from her. Her soft, delicate skin flushed and she pulled back. He'd thought for a moment she would kiss him, the way she almost touched him, the tilt of her head.

The idea that his doubts had made him a coward rankled. He didn't want to lose the best chance he'd ever had at securing her fidelity had his heart pounding. He reached up, cupped her soft jaw and halted her back-peddling.

"I've wanted you since that day in high school when we kissed just before the Christmas break. You were wearing a multi-colored scarf you'd knitted and had a bit of paint smeared on your cheek from art class. You'd been worried about how so many of the girls had let themselves be caught by the boys under the mistletoe in the common room and didn't want to be the only one unkissed."

"You remember that?" she said, shocked.

He smiled gently. "There's very little I don't remember when it comes to you, Sal. I didn't quite love you back then, but I knew I loved you when you studied for that year in Paris. I couldn't have missed an arm or my leg more had I lost it. Only the fact you wrote weekly letters to me made it bearable."

Sally scooted closer and sat in his lap. He loved the comfortable fit of her, the way her body seemed curved perfectly to make him lose his mind. Rob wrapped his arms around her, drawing her to him. She rested her head on his shoulder.

"I never told a soul," she said, her words vibrating along his chest, "but I was so homesick I often felt physically ill. I loved that gap year. I learned more about myself, my dreams and goals and free-handed sketching in those twelve months than I have in the twelve years since. Lots of the styles and people I met influence my paintings, but oh...I missed London, my home, my friends. And you, Bobby. I was so mad when you didn't write back for those first few months, and then when you finally broke down and started corresponding with me it was like I could breathe again. I still missed home, but like you said, it was bearable then."

Rob pressed a finger under her chin and tilted her head back.

"I've still got those letters and every postcard you've ever sent me from your shorter trips," he confessed.

When she nodded, murmured, "Me too" he knew his fate was sealed.

No one else would ever fill this place in his life or heart—no one except his Sal.

Bending forward, he then pressed his lips to hers, kissing her tenderly.

The last of his icy control melted in the heat they generated. Years of cravings, pent-up desire and longing rushed through him. This was not the fiery passion of new love, nor the flash-flame of a lusty fling. This was the slow, true burn of a well-banked, firmly founded love that would never alter course or fade away.

Without moving his lips, Rob slid his arms around her and lifted her to his chest. He stood up. From long years of visits and familiarity, he slowly carried his love up the curving stairs and into her tiny bedroom.

Chapter Two

Rob lay Sally down on her bed and crouched above her while he kicked off his shoes then pulled off his shirt and socks. Her eyes wide, she watched him, her pupils dilated so far that only the thinnest rim of green shined through. Breathing hard, he wanted nothing more than to strip her naked and ravish every inch of her body as he had longed to do, dreamt of for far too long.

Neither of them were virgins, both had a few relationships in their past, but in this moment, Rob felt as eager as that seventeen-year-old boy he'd once been. The last time they'd almost made love he'd been so young, clumsy. He wasn't that boy anymore—far from it. He drew in a deep, shuddering breath and forced some of his control back into place.

Cupping both hands around her jaw, he then let his fingers stroke the smooth stretch of her cheeks and neck. Rob kissed her slowly once more.

"I want this to be perfect," he murmured. He only pulled back only far enough to talk, grazing his lips over her mouth when he formed the words. "I've fantasized about this so often I need to make it good for you and not rush."

"Bobby, you're not the only one here with years of pent-up need. I can see how you've cared for me, how protective a friend you are. You just never showed me the true depth to your feelings, so I always hid my love for you. I'm just as hungry as you for this."

"I never wanted to drag you into the darkness. I try and fix the ugliness around us all. I try and get some justice in this crazy world. You're so different to everything I face at work. We're opposites in so many ways."

"Robert Stevens," Sally choked on her laughter.

He thought there might be mild outrage in her tone, but his brain wasn't as sharp as usual.

"I'm not some sweet little virgin princess who'll be bruised from sleeping on a pea or has waited meekly in her castle for Prince Charming to come along and rescue her. I won't insult your intelligence and bullshit you into thinking I'm some hardened, sassy wise-arse, but I certainly won't shatter and break because someone swears in my direction. I'm not going to be terrorized by you being you. You're a protector, a guardian. The darkness doesn't stain you, Bobby. It's not a part of you. That's what you fight against. How can you not see that?"

He was stunned by the way she saw him and his work. And the vehemence with which she insisted she wasn't some blushing ingénue — which despite the strength of her words, he still believed — rendered him speechless for a moment. Rob gently tugged her long-sleeved top off instead of responding. Removing her shoes and socks, he then skimmed her jeans and cotton knickers down her legs. Laying her bare on the bed, he finally let his gaze devour her hungrily. Every decadent inch of her.

He quickly divested himself of his pants then his boxers. He started to tug the duvet and blankets down from the bed.

"No." Sally laid her hand on his, stopping him. "Unless you think you'll get cold, I don't want to hide under the covers. I want everything. I want to see every line of that muscled body of yours and watch the way your eyes speak to me. This is our only first time, and I don't want to wonder later. I want it all in my memory, so I can remember what it looks like when you make love with me."

Rob could only gape at her for a moment, not because of what she'd said, but because he'd never thought anyone, let alone Sal, would want to watch his every move. Her gorgeous green gaze did seem to literally drink him in with those clever artist's eyes. He flushed, somewhat embarrassed now, knowing she'd very likely make sketches later. It was her nature, to recapture special moments. He'd just never thought far enough to think he'd become one.

"Your word you won't make me recognizable in anything you make public," he said, mortified to think of others — strangers — staring at him, soul bared and body brazen. He'd gladly show Sal every inch of his body, mind and soul, but she held his heart. He didn't want his innermost secrets divulged to all and sundry.

Sally nodded. "My word."

Rob chuckled. He could see her seriousness, knew she meant it and wouldn't break her promise, but still her eyes didn't miss a thing.

"I see I shall have to keep you busy, keep those nimble, talented fingers of yours occupied. We'll be fine, Sal," he said as he climbed next to her on the bed.

The double mattress was roomy enough for them both, but side-by-side he could easily reach out both arms and span the length should he need to.

"Listen to you, you charmer," she teased him.

Rob relished the warmth of her arms she wrapped them around him. Grinning, feeling reckless and like he could take on an army singlehandedly, he kissed the tip of her nose. "Telling it how it is," he insisted. "If I were charming you, gorgeous, I'd say how your smile lights a fire in my heart, or how just the act of you looking at me with those large, speaking eyes of yours has my blood pumping hard and heating my cock."

She laughed, her eyes sparkling.

Rob ruffled her short hair and pressed a hot kiss to her neck, nibbling a slow path down, then along her collar bone. She shivered and clung to him. He loved the sensation.

"Don't ever doubt how that smile of yours does light up my world, though," he murmured. "I can't count the number of times I've picked you up to drag you out for food just to spend some time with you. I enjoy listening to the happy tone in your voice, and that laugh of yours can lighten my mood any time. You complete me, Sal."

Sally grabbed his shoulders, twined her legs around his waist and lifted herself to press her breasts into him. He groaned when she closed her hand around his cock. Already half hard just from staring at her luscious body, his cock ignited under her touch.

"You give me strength. Knowing you're out there, and others like you, like El, makes me feel safer. Every painting I create is to try and bring some joy and passion to others like you. People who need some magic and beauty in their lives."

Her words, as much as her caresses, had him stiffening. Sally moved her hands, pumping up and down to his root. He swelled and thickened. Groaning, he kissed her hungrily, pushing his mouth hard at her, nipping his teeth lightly at her full lips as she drove him to distraction.

Pulling away reluctantly, Rob leaned back then moved to his side so he could reach out and grapple with the top drawer of her bedside table.

"Condoms are in the second drawer," she told him.

He cursed. "Damn it, we're going to move them to the top next time," he groused. He had to shift farther away from the luscious warmth of her body to reach down to the next drawer. Pulling the whole box out, he then tore off a foil packet and left the rest on the top of the table.

"I'll go on the pill," she promised and helped him sheath himself.

Pleased, but wanting it to be her decision when her head was clear, Rob remained silent. He lowered his hand and stroked his fingers out to check she was truly aroused. Her lips were slick and when he caressed his index finger over her clit, her hips arched up. She moaned in approval.

Rob rolled onto his back, lifted Sally up and helped her to straddle him.

"I want to watch you too," he said huskily. "Play with your breasts, gorgeous. They're the perfect handful, pert and round. I want to see how you like them toyed with. I can learn from you."

"Damn, Bobby, you're going to kill me with need," she moaned, fluttering her eyes shut.

Rob watched her, his mouth dry with wanting as she obeyed. She moved over him while he continued to stimulate her clit, penetrating his fingers gently into her pussy as she cupped herself.

After a short time, they were both panting, the chemistry in the room electric and tense.

"Please," she pleaded. "Bobby, please. Don't make me wait longer, I've been patient enough."

"But we're only beginning," he taunted her. He reached up and stroked a smooth line from between her breasts down the center of her torso. He trailed his fingers down, ending at the indentation of her belly button.

Sally opened her eyes and glared at him, looking absolutely adorable.

"I began this trip back behind the sheds when you protected me from those boys and the hazards of smoking," she snapped impatiently. "I've had more years than I want to consider to be put down to foreplay. I think I deserve some satisfaction."

Chuckling, Rob used the hand slick with her juices to guide her hips, moving his other hand to the base of his dick and angling himself correctly. Her head down, still watching him avidly, Sally pressed the palms of her hands onto his shoulders, bracing herself while he placed the tip of his erection at the head of her entrance. Sighing deeply, he breeched her, slowly, slowly easing his cock into her depths.

Sally's head fell back, and she closed her eyes again. Rob sucked in a harsh breath, heat enveloping around his dick as she accepted him inside her body. Farther and farther he moved in, her passage tightly clamping over him. For a moment he thought he might have been wrong, that she was a virgin and he was about to pierce her hymen and cause her pain. She was so tight he couldn't believe she'd had a lover, despite the fact they'd spoken in vague terms of such things before.

But he continued inside her, until after what felt like an eternity, he was fully enveloped by her pussy, balls deep inside her. They stayed steady, Rob rigid with the need to hold still and let her acclimatize to his girth and length. Sally panted harshly, her pale skin flushed and a few beads of sweat making her glow like a goddess.

Wanting to ease her into her pleasure, Rob reached to cup her breasts and gently, tenderly, he toyed with her nipples. She arched her back, thrusting her peaks harder into his grasp. Rolling her tips between thumb and forefinger, he played with her until she started rocking on his cock. Rob kept one hand on her breast but lowered the other until he could cup her hip and hold her steady while she moved up and down, fucking herself on his cock.

The pleasure rippling through his body was intense, delicious in its power. A hard knot of hunger twisted in his stomach, his balls rising as the tension from her movements grew. Soon, he tugged Sally to bend over him so he could lift his chest up and suck at her teat. Scraping his teeth lightly over the sensitive nub, he suckled her hard. She shuddered in pleasure, her spine arching wantonly.

Need crawled over his skin and he canted his hips upwards, thrusting his length deeper into Sal, the force of each movement growing.

"More, Bobby, please," she panted.

She lowered her head and they kissed hungrily. She nipped him with her teeth and they tangled their tongues around each other. Gone was the tender, delicate touches of before, now he was as desperate as she, driven to the brink by the force of their passion.

He roamed his hands over her slick skin. Their bodies slapped together as they each took from the other. Rob had no idea when he moaned or she sighed, but the noise of their pleasure echoed out across the loft and filled the air. They raced toward climax. Finally, Rob could feel the pressure get the best of him—he knew he'd not last much longer.

"Gorgeous," he panted. "I'm almost there."

"Thank fuck. Just a little more."

He moved his mouth to suckle at the other breast. Her nipple was a hard point he rolled lightly between his teeth before drawing down on it and sucking. He stroked his fingers over her clit. He felt her body tighten, and her pussy clamped down hard around his shaft, caressing it like a vice. She panted a couple of quick, breathless gasps. Arching farther back, her breast pressed against his mouth and she screamed.

Her body convulsed and the pulses detonated his climax. Rob grasped her hips, holding her steady so she wouldn't fall while he thrust with abandon. Unable to restrain himself a moment longer, he plunged into her, shouting out his release. He ejaculated over and over. He emptied himself into the condom, pumping with his dick as he came through his orgasm.

Just as suddenly as his pleasure overrode him, he fell down the other side of the peak and crashed. Every muscle in his body sagged back into the mattress. Exhaustion washed over him. Breathing hard, they both sounded like they'd sprinted a mile. Sally gingerly pulled herself off him. About to stop her, he quietened when she wrapped an arm snugly around his waist and appeared to find a more comfortable position.

Rob pressed a kiss to her cheek, then her forehead, then her mussed hair, which now spiked out in every direction.

"I love you, Sal," he murmured sleepily.

"I love you too, Bobby," she whispered.

Feeling sated and relaxed, complete like he'd never been before, Rob drew Sal into the warmth and safety of his embrace and closed his eyes just for a second or two.

* * * *

Rob snapped his eyes open. His brain clicked immediately into gear as if someone had turned a switch back on.

For a moment he couldn't recall anything. He shifted defensively. A warm body was pressed against him, an arm around his waist. He wasn't dating anyone. Rob knew there was only one person who held his heart. So why was his arm wrapped around a warm, naked...*oh*.

Memory flooded back and the world righted on its axis.

The painting.

El and James.

Sally.

Sally.

Rob drew Sal tighter and kissed the sensual, exposed length of her neck. She murmured incoherently. Sally smiled in that perfect, devastating way he adored. Her eyes were languid, a dark, mossy green that seemed to hold the secrets of nations within them. Her teeth flashed, gorgeous, straight and white. Sal's grin, that brilliance that shined from her sweet soul always felt warmer than the sun to him.

"Hey there, sleepyhead," she teased.

He grinned back instinctively, but then her words registered.

Sleepyhead?

His head snapped around and he turned his upper body so he could stare at her digital alarm clock.

Holy fuck. He'd lost an hour.

Sure, he had been woken up at three a.m. and had worked all the way through till well past lunch time, but he couldn't afford to sleep when it was still early in the afternoon.

"Shit. Damn," he cursed. He scrambled from the bed. Crossing the room, he then hurried into the tiny en suite to remove the condom and quickly rinse his body. "I need to call El—hell, she's been on her own for hours now. I need to write my report. I have to find that fucking painting. And understand what this whole bloody mess means. I need to—"

"You need to not carry the burden of the world on your shoulders," Sally insisted in a soft but firm tone.

Rob rushed back into the bedroom without a word. He grabbed his boxers and turned to her as he slid them on. She was rumpled, flushed and looking gorgeously disheveled only half covered by the sheet. He wondered if he was completely ruining her post-sex glow.

He knelt on the bed and drew her close then kissed her slowly.

"I swear I don't mean to be an ogre," he promised as he stood. He flicked his gaze down to his pants, turned them the right way around so he could put them on properly. "I didn't mean to fall asleep. I was just so relaxed, the moment was so perfect. And you were there, all warm and stunning from our sex and—dammit."

Rob cringed internally to think of how he appeared, rushing to leave his lover's bed after their first time having sex. Hopping on one foot to get dressed in seconds instead of minutes. He'd be lucky if Sal ever let him into her bed again. Rob shook his head, not able to even contemplate that scenario.

"Sal, I'm sorry. This case will do my head in. I don't mean to rush off, but I must. I just can't get a handle on the situation, and losing an hour to sleep is just time I don't have right now."

"And I'm not being much help." Sally nodded.

Rob shook his head firmly as he buttoned his pants. "Don't say that. You've given me plenty to think about. I just—"

"You need to stop carrying this weight alone. Bobby, you're not contaminated by your profession, or the only person who can do this. El is almost as strong as you, and a bloody good partner. You've told me so hundreds of times. And while I understand you see a harsher side to the world than most people, it doesn't change who you are, especially to me. In your soul, you're still the same Bobby who helped guide me through the final years of school."

Rob stopped buttoning his shirt at the insistent tone in her voice.

Sally climbed from the bed. She reached out, grabbed his hands in hers and held him still for a moment. "You came to me so I could give you my knowledge and experience. You wanted my help. For heavens' sake, let me give it to you."

Rob paused for a moment, weighing things in his mind. He felt torn. It was true—he needed help and plenty of it. And while part of him still rebelled at dragging Sally deeper into the murkier depths of his world, she was right. He respected her, loved her. If she was adamant she wanted to do this who was he to stop her? Especially when he needed the assistance.

Protecting her was second nature for him, but she was not weak or a coward. He could still watch over her while she worked side-by-side with him. Part of him even wanted that.

"I won't be able to keep the guys off you if you come to the office with me like this," he teased her. Kissing her tenderly, because he was now free to do so, Rob wrapped her in a warm hug then lifted her off the ground. She wound her arms behind his neck. She twined her legs around his waist and even after the cold water and bloody good shag they'd just had, his cock twitched in his pants.

He lowered Sally back to the floor and kissed her one last time.

"I'll go downstairs and check my messages. Meet you there."

Sally nodded. He moved to climb back down the stairs when he felt her hand lightly slap his arse. Choking, he turned half around and tilted his head at her. The vixen's eyes gleamed, pride and humor shining in their depths. Sal sniggered and sashayed into the bathroom. Rob would have bet a year's salary the extra wriggle in her hips and buttocks were very much on purpose and for his benefit.

After a moment, he heard the water running.

"I've unleashed a demon," he muttered happily to himself as he went back downstairs. "A succubus, or maybe a fiery temptress from hell. I'm doomed."

Rob crossed the large room. He went to the coffee table where he'd left his leather folder earlier when he and Sal had become...distracted. His work case had a custom-made pocket in the leather, which was where he usually stashed his phone.

As he passed one of the easels, he noticed it was the lightly sketched one he hadn't been able to make out properly earlier. Curious, Rob paused and glanced at it now the opportunity had risen. Gray pencil had been used sparingly, so it was still hard to guess exactly what the picture was and how it would turn out. He thought he saw the outlines of a man and woman, hands linked, walking with their backs to the viewer.

Clearly Sally was still trying to block in the pieces, possibly even unsure herself what the outcome would be. The man seemed to have a circle near him, even fainter outlines that could be buildings or trees...or, hell, almost anything in the distant horizon toward where they led.

Rob was intrigued, his imagination already provoked at just the faintest outline. He shook his head, clearing it of the whimsy and forcing himself back to reality. Knowing Sally, the picture might take a dozen turns before she worked out what she wanted the piece to be. Even then, she'd go over the sketch again in charcoal to firm up the main strokes and details and only then would she start to paint. The final product could be completely different to this hazy outline.

He continued toward the table. Pulling his mobile free, he then flipped it to check the screen. He winced.

Three missed calls and two voicemails.

Damn. He hoped he hadn't left the Agency — or El in particular — in the lurch. His heart beating fast, he pressed a couple of buttons and checked his messages.

"Rob, it's El. Just a heads up for you — Louise Calloway is likely headed into HQ to check on her brother. Neither James nor I think she's involved in this, though I do think she knows more than she's told us about the work he does in general. I gave her my card and the main reception number we give out to civilians. I'll call you back when I know more. Be safe."

Rob stared thoughtfully out of the window for a moment, analyzing the information and assimilating it. If El didn't think Luke Calloway's sister was involved, chances were his partner's instincts were sound. A part of his mind cheered to learn El and James were working together, he'd need to check on that and assure himself El was comfortable and happy, but mostly Rob tried to juggle the puzzle pieces he had.

Partially distracted, he played the second message.

"Rob, it's El. We've found it! The...erm, painting."

He chuckled at this. Obviously excited, El had forgotten general Agency protocol, which was to leave as little incriminating data as possible over unsecured lines. Rob grinned, bursting with pride for her.

"Look, I know you need a break, some sleep, but seriously. We've got it. James and I are heading back to HQ. There was a safe in the target's flat. It's complicated, but we've recovered what we need. Get back to me soon."

Rob didn't like the sound of 'it's complicated', but he knew that could turn out to mean practically anything.

"Is everything okay?" Sally leaned her head on his shoulder and wrapped her arms around his waist.

Rob hugged her close with one hand, amazed she'd managed to freshen up and dress so quickly.

"El and James found the painting," he replied excitedly. "The message is only half an hour old, so they're likely almost back at the office. I need to go in."

"I can come with you," she offered. "Not just because after all these years I'd enjoy seeing more than the reception foyer, but because I might be able to offer some insight. If I can get a close look at the piece there could be something I'd notice, or understand, that you and El could possibly miss."

Rob had to squash the instinct to simply say no. He didn't want Sally in danger, or anywhere near the men responsible for so much damage to the city. He needed to acknowledge to himself, though, that it wasn't purely for him to decide these things. Part of him longed to wrap her up in cotton wool, protect her and keep her safe. But at heart she was a free spirit, and if he smothered her it would end badly for them both.

The Agency headquarters was in the middle of central London. It was well guarded and a little known secret outside of select circles. Taking up numerous floors of a stately old building, it seemed from the outside like all the other corporate offices filled with normal people going about their normal business.

There were few safer places he could take her. Keeping her out of this was needless and selfish — even if his motives were pure and noble.

Reluctantly, he nodded.

Sally beamed happily at him and tightened her arms around him again in a big hug. Neither of them spoke for a moment. Rob forced himself not to say anything to spoil her moment. This went against his instincts, but he couldn't deny that beautiful beam of pleasure. Rob was grateful, not only for Sally's understanding, but also for her kindness in giving him a moment to mentally come to grips with the change in their relationship.

He took a deep breath and reminded himself it would work out fine.

"Bet you ten quid the laboratory analysts will be drooling all over the painting," he teased, trying hard to lighten the mood. "I'm sure they'll be begging to run tests and take samples. You think that we become conspiracy nuts after a bottle or two of wine, well I gotta warn you, Sal, these guys live and breathe the stuff. Hidden encryptions, secret messages and underground movements to radically alter the world. This is their bread and butter, what they live for."

"Joke all you like, Bobby, but I can see your unease. I trust you. If you say it's genuinely too dangerous, I'll step back. But you came here for my help and I want to give it. Besides, this is exciting. It's thrilling to see even a small slice of what you do every day."

It was clear how eager she was to start on what he suspected she saw was a grand adventure. It was written all over her. She bounced lightly on the balls of her feet, and her eyes shined. Rob had to stop himself from swearing when he noticed the anticipation in her beautiful green gaze. He so rarely saw her this excited—normally it was only when she painted that her passions were so freely unleashed.

Her sensual, vivid reaction to this situation had his body reacting to her beauty. He kissed the top of her head, loving the faintly floral shampoo she used.

"You charm everyone you meet," he said. "I'm sure the lab guys will love having you around. Their conversation might go a little over your head, but I bet you can have a lot of really important input into their tests. Besides, El will be thrilled to see me bring you along. She's been nudging me to let my guard down with you forever."

"I always knew El was a brilliant woman," Sally replied with a happy smile. "Let me grab my bag and we can go in. You're practically vibrating with the need to get moving. On the drive into your office, you can fill me in on El and James."

Sally turned and walked to a large chest of drawers. In the past, Rob knew she used the furniture as storage for all manner of tools and artist things that came in handy sporadically. Now and then he'd see her rummage through it for various items. This time, she pulled out a magnifying glass and placed it into a small bag. Sal was murmuring to herself, so he simply watched her. She continued to open and shut various drawers and stacked up a few items to take with her.

Finally, she collected her keys, purse and phone, slung the bag over her shoulder and seemed ready. Rob sent a quick text to El telling her he and Sally were on their way in. Collecting his leather folder, Rob then crossed the room and met Sally at the door. Unable to help himself, he cupped her jaw and bent down. She stood up on her toes to meet him and they shared an eager kiss.

Rob stroked the back of his fingers over her dark locks of hair. He brushed them from her eyes, even though he knew in a moment they'd fall back across her brow. He gazed into her face and admired her for the millionth time.

"Now that's the way every day should start," he commented.

She laughed, grabbed his arse and gave a little squeeze.

"Absolutely," she agreed as she opened the door. Dancing a little on her toes, she jiggled her way down onto the footpath.

Rob chuckled at her—couldn't help himself. He checked the door locked behind them, pulling on the handle to make sure no one could just waltz in. It didn't surprise him Sally hadn't made certain herself — her faith was astounding.

Rob followed his love out onto the street, deeply amused.

Chapter Three

"Rob!" El called from across the room.

Sally could hear the surprise in the redhead's tone and it made her grin. When Rob paused, Sally did too. She loved how he pressed his hand on her shoulder. He was watching El, clearly curious about what she had to tell him, but his light touch indicated for her to wait while he dealt with something.

Even though his focus was clearly on his co-worker, some part of him still remained on her, almost as if it were instinctive. It made her feel as if they were a couple.

They'd been friends for so many years and some things, she knew, would only deepen between them. Sally could guess that there might be a few passionate 'discussions' on boundaries, and other things as they both adjusted to this new, wonderful intimacy between them. But she loved the solid, warm weight of Rob's touch, even the casual, unthinking guidance that he gave now.

Her chest warmed. She felt precious, protected.

Sally grinned brightly at El. They were genuinely friends and liked each other immensely. Rob also grinned at his partner, but Sally jumped in first. Happiness bubbled up inside her, despite the circumstances, and she needed to share that with another person.

"El, look at how gorgeous you are," Sally gushed, rushing over to embrace the agent.

They hugged, and El chuckled.

"You're full of it," El replied saucily. "I'm sleep deprived, starving and exhausted. What happened to that artist's eye of yours?"

Sally smiled, feeling a bit smug. It *was* her artist's eye that had caught the details. Details like the faint flush of happiness only a sexually sated woman could hold. The angle of El's body which leaned very slightly toward the sandy-haired man El had stood next to when Sally and Rob had entered the room. The way El clearly sparkled with love for that same man.

Both women glanced up as Rob crossed over and shook hands with the blond man.

"Who is he and how long have you been with him? I didn't know you were seeing anyone," Sally said in a lower tone.

Surprise then resignation crossed El's face.

"An old friend," El replied. "James. He's... It's... We're... It's complicated, okay?"

"My favorite kind of story." Sally nodded. "Later?"

"Promise," El said with clear relief.

Sally was prepared to let her off the hook for now, but she wondered what story was behind the flush and inner glow El all but shined with.

"Congratulations on finding the painting, that's amazing work," Rob was saying as El and Sally came closer.

"El was responsible for most of it," James insisted.

"I think you've both done an amazing job. I can't wait to see it," Sally interjected.

"I'm pleased Rob finally broke down and came to you for help. He can be stubborn as a rock sometimes," El said with a smile.

"Nothing could keep me away once I got the story from him," Sally said. "This sounds like amazing fun. I brought some tools. Bobby mentioned you have a lab here, but I can't imagine they're used to dealing with centuries old, priceless pieces of art. Is there someone in particular I need to be sweet to? I don't want to step on toes."

"I've left the painting with Ben in the lab," El said.

Sally looked from El to Rob, then smiled at James. "Hi, I'm Sally. I'm with Rob."

"James. I'm with El, though I'm sort of a part-time consultant here, too."

"The Agency takes on consultants?" Sally asked. She gave Rob a part outraged, part excited glance. The rascal had never even hinted she could become safely involved on a casual basis with his work. She made a mental note to seriously research it very soon.

She knew she'd have a twinkle in her eyes as she held Rob's gaze for a moment.

"Really?" Sally drew out the word so it was clearly full of promise and undeniable interest. "Well, maybe I should have a quiet word with you later, James, and see if you can give me a few pointers on how to wrangle such a position with these guys. Obviously Bobby's been a little too closed-mouthed recently."

"Hey, I didn't drag my feet over bringing you in here today," he said defensively.

Sally laughed, linked her arm through his and held his hand. She twined her fingers amongst his and squeezed a little. Their gazes met and although she made sure to smile at him, show him she was mostly teasing, she knew he'd see the stubborn tilt to her jaw. She loved Bobby with all her heart. Her whole body still sang from their love-making earlier and not for anything in this world would she take back the deepening on their relationship.

But neither would she be swaddled and set aside, pushed out of any situation she could genuinely help out in. She was different, thought along non-linear lines and she wouldn't pretend for a second that she was cut out for the life and work Bobby and El were made for. But neither would she run and hide, or bow out of something she could assist with.

"You might not have dragged your feet *today*, Bobby. But it only took the recovery of a stolen painting and...what? Eleven years? Twelve? That you've been working here. Still, I suppose the old adage of better late than never certainly fits here."

Sal chuckled. She gave his hand a final, tender squeeze then let go. She didn't want to push him or embarrass him in front of his colleagues. She had no idea if he'd feel uncomfortable with her touching him for more than a few seconds here at work and didn't want to make him ill at ease. When she moved her hand, she noticed Bobby turned his shoulders and tilted them slightly.

They remained close enough that they touched.

Sally smiled, she could feel herself glow happily.

"I sense there's no correct response to this." James shot Rob an amused look.

Rob chuckled. "We're both doomed. It'll likely be easier to accept it now than drag it out," he agreed.

"Eleanor, Robert, I hear you've done us proud." Gary Waldron came toward them.

"Actually, sir —" Rob started, but El sent him a quick glare and he cut himself off sharply.

Sally remained silent but felt her eyes widen. Was Rob meant to have been with El and James but stuck with her instead? She filed the information away to review later.

"This is James Waters and Sally Langtry. They've also been helping Rob and me with the investigation," El spoke over Rob, effectively shutting him up.

Handshakes were exchanged and El continued. "We were actually just on our way to the laboratory. Ben's had the piece almost twenty minutes now and we feel Sally might be able to offer some insight."

"Fantastic. I just wanted to congratulate you all. I'm sorry I can't stay, but I'm already late for a teleconference with the mayor and a few others who have been breathing fire throughout the day. At least the recovery of the Cezanne will put out a lot of complaints and angst. I'll expect your reports soon."

When Waldron was out of ear shot, Rob shot a firm glance to El. "El, I can't write a report for something I wasn't a party to," he insisted.

"Of course not, I know better than to fudge something like that," she replied sharply in a low tone. "But neither do you have to admit to his face you weren't there. I could see you about to fall on your sword. You've been working just as hard as I have and we're a team. Besides, we have the painting, that's all that matters."

"Ben Demmens and his team have the painting," Rob corrected his partner.

Sally could see the tension around his eyes and mouth, tiny muscles that tightened only when he wasn't happy. She guessed he felt upset, or perhaps guilty, but he seemed willing to let it go for now.

"Come on, let's all go have a look before the Gallery or a bunch of dignitaries from the mayor try to beat down our door and take it back," El said.

Sally jumped very slightly when Rob rested his hand on her shoulder. She tilted her head up to look at him. He gave her a small smile, barely a shadow of the one she'd awoken with just a short time ago. Trying to reassure him with her gaze, she smiled at him. A faint tingle of happiness and sexual chemistry shivered through her as Bobby gently guided her down a corridor. El and James walked ahead of them, having left as soon as Rob finished his sentence.

The simmering, electric attraction seemed to only grow between herself and Rob, even while they moved down the hallway. She wondered if subconsciously the tension of knowing how important this work would be, of how many lives might potentially be affected, was only adding to the weight of the moment and intensifying her feelings. Sally knew without a doubt she loved Rob, and had done so for a very long time. But never had the light press of his hand on her clothed body, and a casual walk hit her so strongly, either.

She cleared her throat, forced her mind to remain on what was happening and not the emotional rollercoaster she appeared to have climbed upon.

"Do you really have laboratory facilities here?" Sally questioned. She tried to focus on their surroundings, her mind and attention soon distracted by the sedate, very professional and particularly soulless offices they seemed to be striding past. Looking around, she drank in the sights of Bobby's work. Inspiration often struck her from the oddest things.

Exposed beams painted mission brown and a drab shade of taupe covered the walls. Everything seemed to be 'old skool' and practically dripping in many decades-old interior design. At first she hadn't liked it much at all, but she realized there was a calm feel to it, a solidarity in the knowledge that the people within this place were here, protecting her country, for decades. It led to the belief that even decades in the future they would still be here — or somewhere similar to here — performing their duty.

Rob indicated the frosted glass double doors at the end of the hall.

"Ah," Sally murmured to herself.

Internal security cameras were mounted above the doors, three that she could see. Sally tried to gauge whether there'd be any blind spots, but it was difficult for her to judge. To her, they seemed to cover every inch of the hallway. The keypad on the wall appeared state of the art. Clearly when it came to their security everything was very top line. Modern technology was now well in evidence.

Understated, traditional wealth filled the offices she'd been in, opulent, unashamed expense and technology clearly reigned, at least in this corner of the Agency.

"It was easier to create a small lab on site, rather than have us commute back and forth to somewhere outside the city," Rob explained. "Especially since all too frequently, time is a critical factor in any job we're doing. We're not equipped for some of the more specialist testing that sometimes occurs, but our technicians can jerry-rig almost anything pretty quickly. And have other experts or equipment couriered in at a moment's notice. To date we've never had something we couldn't handle — and I hope we never do."

El and James remained a pace back from the door. El and Rob looked silently at each other for a moment. El waved her hand to the door with a small smile. Sally watched as Rob stepped up to the keypad and after a moment's pause typed in a complicated sequence of numbers.

Sally blinked, stunned. Although she hadn't counted, it had seemed like the pass code had been twenty or even more numbers long. She knew full well she was not some mathematical genius, or even particularly savvy when it came to that sort of thing. But between her work and personal email accounts, her three bank accounts and her parents' security code alarms and her two PINs, she often had to resort to little rhymes and memory tricks to recall a given security number. And that didn't even include phone numbers and the like.

For the first time ever, she wondered if her oldest and dearest friend was even more of a superhero than she'd already believed him to be.

Rob seemed to catch her impressed glance.

A small beep signaled his password had been accepted and presumably recorded. He held the door open for them and Sally stepped forward, caught somewhere between surprise and wonder. She lifted her eyebrows and gave him a cheeky grin as they entered.

"I was muttering a rhyme," Rob whispered.

Sally chuckled, still charmed by his skills.

She entered the large area and, after a few steps to make room for the others, stopped suddenly. The room was enormous and had clearly been renovated in the not-too-distant past. It appeared as if a number of offices had been demolished, the interior ripped back to the structural bones and a large, airy, thoroughly modern lab built in its place.

Work benches were laid out in an orderly manner, some scrupulously clean, others cluttered with numerous cool-looking — but mystifying — pieces of equipment. Sally couldn't even name most of them, but she could tell this was a place of learning. It had that light, positive feel to it. Answers were found here. Puzzles solved.

Three men in lab coats were gathered around an island bench. A large lamp shined brightly onto the canvas spread out on the table.

"We couldn't possibly flake off some paint samples."

"Oh, come on, like they'd ever know."

"Maybe we should. I've read that latent irradiation in many of the older lead-based paints — "

"We are *not* taking samples, Thompson. End of discussion. Now, perhaps if we — "

El cleared her throat. One of the men lifted his head, then the others followed suit. They all had varying degrees of guilt written across their faces.

"Ben, let me introduce James Waters and Sally Langtry. They're both consulting with us and have come to help with the Cezanne."

"A pleasure," Ben said as they exchanged handshakes. "This is George and Tim."

"I've brought some tools I thought might be helpful," Sally said. For a moment she felt the smallest bit shy. She was an artist, and a damn fine one too, but for the first time in forever she wondered if she was out of her league.

Not wanting to step on toes, or offend the technicians, she nevertheless did feel she could contribute. Sally smiled, only a little uncertain of herself. Ben seemed to stare at her for a moment, but then the small amount of resistance in his stance softened.

A minute later James, Sally, Ben, George and Tim all hovered over the painting, discussing various techniques animatedly. Rob and El leaned back against a different bench next to each other, watching.

"A polarizing light, if we refract if correctly, might uncover differences in the pigments and then we could—"

"But infra-red light would surely be better. That spectrum is far broader and—"

In one small portion of her brain, Sally noticed El and Rob leaning in and talking softly to each other. She'd never been so aware of another person before. Even so, she had no real interest in trying to overhear what they spoke about—this puzzle consumed her and she wanted a hand in solving it.

"I don't know about you, mate, but I don't want to be the one to try and get approval to take a sample from this. The sheer value of this artwork would mean we'd have to wait for insurance paperwork, and likely many levels of managers and who knows what else just to take a gram or more. It might be something to consider if we come up empty on other thoughts though," James added with a shake of his head. "But I do like the idea of running the canvas under different light sources. What if the reason so many people have interest in it is because it's been altered in some way?"

"Oh, I like that idea." Sally brightened, her mind taking James' suggestion in a few different directions. She'd read a number of very interesting tomes on the best forgers throughout the ages, and her mind scrambled to keep pace with the vivid discussion.

"May I?" She raised a hand-held magnifier and looked around the assembled men.

They nodded and shuffled to give her room. Sally bent low over the table, the glass scant inches from the painting. Starting at the nearest corner and working her way up and down the length of the painting, Sally examined the piece in minute detail. The men continued to discuss tests amongst themselves, though she could feel the weight of their attention still on her as she made her painstakingly slow progress.

"Hmm," Sally murmured, caught at a particular point. She ran her gaze in a grid pattern over the tiny section, first up and down, then side to side. It was a frequently taught method of systematically searching an art piece, seeing each section both horizontally and vertically and also covering the area twice. It was tedious, but a very thorough way to search.

Sally even moved her body, trying to catch the various refractions of light. Studying the painting this intently, she tried to discover if her eyes were playing tricks or if she'd really found something.

Her mind racing with the possibilities, she glanced up. To give herself a break, Sally allowed her eyes to become unfocused as she turned inward, making a judgment call.

"Mmm, James," she said after a moment, then held out the magnifier. "What do you think of this area in the background, the grassy hill?"

"The brushstrokes definitely appear different," he said immediately.

He didn't bend to peer closer, but Sally could tell from the avid, intense way he stared that the small section of canvas had his entire concentration.

"Oh, definitely, I could see that. But are you familiar with Vi—the restorer's work? I want a second opinion before I put forward any hypothesis."

"Wait," El snapped as she pushed away from the bench. "The painting has been tampered with? But there hasn't been time."

"Hang on," James said calmly, not even glancing back at El.

Rob snickered and didn't seem the least fazed when El shot him a glare.

The room was silent while James studied the painting for a minute, then two, going over the same small area. Sally was happy to be still and wait. This would be important, and just as she'd refused to rush, she couldn't imaging James taking anything less than all the time he needed to make his decision too.

She looked to her lover, and unusually Rob seemed to fidget, appearing impatient. For a moment she thought maybe he was uncomfortable. Rob was always the soul of patience and even-tempered. It wasn't until she glanced at the clock that she realized James had been studying the painting for almost five minutes now. Amused, despite the seriousness of the situation, Sally beamed at Rob, trying to convey she thought this was good news and something positive.

James stood up and stretched his back.

"I definitely recognize the work of this woman," James finally agreed. He passed the glass back to Sally. "She only works for a select group of clients, though, and has been semi-retired these last few years. Careful, delicate work like this doesn't happen in a few hours, or even a few days. There's no way this occurred since the heist. It has to have been before that."

"It's been in the possession of the National Gallery for a number of years," Ben insisted. "Though it's only been on show for a month or so. But that's not unusual, museums and galleries frequently have thousands of pieces, the vast majority of which usually are in storage."

"Let's try it under infra-red," Tim said.

Ben grasped what appeared to be a hand-held electrical wand, brandishing it about like a mini sword. George moved next to the doors and switched off a bank of lights. Three quarters of the laboratory fell into darkness. Tim fiddled with the light and ran it over the painting. Hard as she looked, Sally couldn't see the markings she'd hoped to find.

Rapidly blinking, she tried to ignore the small ache of eye strain and redoubled her efforts. No one else spoke, and when Ben reached the spot where they'd begun, he didn't even pause but continued straight on into a second round.

Sally's stomach sank. The fact no one had stopped to point something out meant it possibly wasn't just her. No one else had seen anything either.

Patiently, she peered as best she could. The minutes ticked by. After the third painfully slow pass, Ben seemed to admit defeat. A small click sounded as he turned off the device. The technician stood and heaved a sigh.

"Okay," Sally said, undaunted, "I have an ultraviolet light. Let me try that."

The process began again.

This time it only took a few minutes for tiny anomalies to show. Sally put the speed down to them now knowing what they were looking for, and already having an area to focus upon. It was like narrowing down the haystack, there was still a lot to sift through, but they were making progress.

At first Sally thought she was going cross-eyed, but then she realized it was a kind of dot pattern.

"Wait—" She held out a finger, pointing.

At the exact same moment James said, "I think I see —"

They all grinned at each other, George and Tim nodding furiously. Without a word they all leaned in closer, their heads practically touching.

Ben still held the light source out steadily, guiding the wand around as they each showed him what they saw. Brainstorming together, they gesticulated, their voices rising when the excitement mounted in the room — the thrill of discovery.

"...and look up here, these dots in the sky. They're not original either."

"Ben, grab that pen and paper you mentioned and I'll read out the letters to you," James said.

"I want to get a closer look at these dots," Sally added, murmuring. They reminded her of something and it was just at the tip of her tongue.

The men bustled about, an eager murmur filling the air as they talked amongst themselves. Like an electric shock, Sally became aware of Rob standing behind her. Significantly taller than her, he peered over her head, his thighs pressed warmly against her, sending a zing of pleasure through her blood.

Sally had frozen, leaning so close to the painting she worried her breath might adversely oxidize the masterpiece, and her nose was pressed against the magnifier. She could tell the second he saw for himself what had gotten them so excited. He raised his eyebrows. Tiny pinpricks of glowing blue light were clearly visible under the small torch she shined on the painting.

"Oh," he interrupted. "I can see that. All those dots in the sky of the painting. What is it? Morse code?"

"Or a substitution enigma. Maybe a letter-slash-symbol code," George suggested.

El came forward, squeezed herself up against James and peered with them.

"Tim, can you please go to the storage lockers," she asked without lifting her gaze from the painting. "I'm pretty certain we have a UV filter for the camera that's kept somewhere around here. I want pictures of this code and the dots. I know you'll want copies to study, and Analysis will need them to work on too, but I don't trust those bastards at the Gallery. They'll pressure the mayor to put weight on management here and retrieve their painting. Once all that bluster and red-tape is passed, we'll never get our hands on this beauty ever again, and they sure as hell won't admit to anything being in the painting, so I want our own documentation kept locked down tight."

"You know, that appears awfully like Orion's belt." James pointed at three glowing dots that were close together at an angle.

"I thought that looked like his body above it, too," El added.

"It's not a code," Sally confirmed. She'd not wanted to say anything, but if both James and El saw what she had, then she wanted to add her weight to their hypothesis and even take it a step further. "Someone has added the constellations. I'd bet that's a map of the sky from a specific point and date. Ingenious, really, to hide that in plain sight."

"Could you please go back to the hill? Yes, there," George muttered while he scrawled notes.

Sally glanced back and forth, from George's notes to the small section of green background she illuminated with her UV light. In neat dots and symbols, George transcribed the code, making notations of where each series of stars, letters and numbers appeared.

It seemed like gibberish to Sally, but she knew enough about Rob and his work that the analysts he sometimes spoke of in a reverent tone would have a field day with it.

"Don't these things usually need a key?" Rob queried as George went back and carefully double checked he had the position and sequence exactly right in his transcription.

"Yes, but it's stupid to not take photos. Surely we want as exact a copy as possible? We'd definitely like to try to crack it ourselves," Ben replied. "I don't like our chances of being able to hold onto the painting above a day, particularly not with the level of pressure Waldron is experiencing from all angles right now. If we have our own copies of everything, at least we won't be behind everyone else. Masters, I know, lives for this sort of stuff. He might be able to crack it, or find the key in the first series of letters — or the last, who knows with these things?"

Tim returned with the camera and a satchel draped over his shoulder.

"I brought all the filters," he puffed, clearly having hurried back.

"That's a good idea," Sally said. "Obviously someone has gone to great pains to carefully add in a vision of the night sky and the coded sequence within the background. I'm beginning to believe they then even paid an exorbitant fee to have it carefully restored after their work was done. It's logical they could well have hidden the key in here too, but under a different form of light so anyone who stumbled upon one clue wouldn't necessarily get another."

"I agree with Miss Langtry here," James added. "I'd try black light. If that doesn't work, maybe we could try the full spectrum of colors next — red, orange, yellow, blue and so on. I have access to various sources of those single-rayed lights, if you need assistance. I know most microbiology and chemistry labs don't usually deal in alternate light sources unless it's on a small slide under a microscope. And since we've already agreed we can't take samples from the painting, we need the lights to be in a torch. That's where knowing some art technicians and restorers will come in handy."

"Do you have them nearby?" Ben asked. "We have most of the filters for the camera and could check the painting that way. But taking so many photos will eat up a lot of our time. If we can look first and only expend effort when we know there's something to capture, that could speed the process up."

"I've got black light here, but I only brought those three with me—IR, UV and black," Sally lamented, wishing she'd known they'd be needed. She hated the thought of time being wasted while James went off site to get what they required, particularly when she had them stored safely back at her studio.

"I can have them within the hour." James cast a quick glance to El.

El nodded at James then turned to Rob.

"I'm going to take you up on that offer to start the report, partner," she said. "James and I will be back as quickly as we can manage."

"I can handle that, don't worry about it. We can follow you out for a moment," Rob said with a meaningful glance at El.

Sally didn't need to be a mind reader to know something else was happening in the background, something she'd evidently missed. But clearly Rob wanted to speak to El about something. Sally was about to turn back to the painting, her mind already sifting through the few things she'd held to herself, but Rob caught her eye. He tilted his head to indicate she follow him.

"Oh," she said and glanced wistfully at the painting. She hated to leave it, especially when she felt certain it held so many more secrets she longed to uncover, but she refused to let Rob down. She took a step toward him only to discover he'd crossed the room to her.

He laid a hand gently on her arm and bent low to speak into her ear.

"If you want to stay that's fine, but I need to ask a favor. It can wait a short while, though," he said softly.

"No. No, I'll come out with you. That's fine," she said.

In a sense she was glad. Sally was fairly certain she knew the restorer personally, and while she didn't want to make a big deal of it out there in the laboratory, she did think it was something Rob and she could follow up on. It was just that simultaneous to this, a part of her had hoped to ogle the delicious artwork some more, too.

Ah well, Sal, can't have everything, can you, girl?

Feeling faintly guilty at her selfish thoughts—time was obviously of the essence here—Sal left the laboratory, following James and El and with Rob coming up behind her. The door locked behind them with a click. The corridor was empty. El scanned the surroundings and Rob leaned left and right to check none of the office doors were open.

For a brief second, Sally felt like she was in some sort of thriller movie, or perhaps a horror. One where after they split the party up, the ax-wielding maniac started chopping the actors into bloody pieces. She shook her head, mentally berating herself to pay attention.

"Okay, I think we've got some privacy," El stated in a rushed manner as she turned to face Rob. "What's up?"

"Sal, you recognized the name of the restorer, or forger, I'm still not sure which yet. Vi, I think you said. Darling, I need you to give me that name. James, you seemed to know him too. I'm thinking if you can give El the details on how and where to recover those light sources, then you can come with me to speak to the restorer and—"

"Hang on, Bobby," Sally interjected, a small frisson of annoyance shaking through her. "That's the favor you were thinking of a minute ago? For me to just give you an address and name and sit here waiting for you? That connection is far more important than what we're doing here. Ben, Tim and George are perfectly capable of taking photos and documenting everything we discover in the painting. I'm interested in this case—and involved now. It's thrilling, finding secret codes hidden in a century-old painting, I won't pretend otherwise, but neither am I going to let you just leave me back here while you go off and solve the puzzle without me. Besides, you won't be able to speak to Vicky without me."

Rob looked from Sally to James. James shrugged.

"I'm not fussed, mate. I needed prodding from Sally, but I, too, thought it was the work of Victoria Parker. She's one of the best. Been semi-retired these last few years. Although she will take the occasional work when her curiosity is roused, or if it's an exceptionally stunning piece, she's not done a lot in recent times. I'm happy to stay with El, meet you both back here."

Rob and Sally looked at each other. Sally set her jaw firmly, not willing to yield on this unless Bobby had a bloody good reason behind him. So far, he'd shown her nothing that would convince her to stay behind, even though she loved the painting and could happily study it for weeks.

That wasn't the point.

"Are you sure?" Rob said.

She could already hear the resignation in his tone.

"You were enjoying yourself so much," he said.

"I'm absolutely sure," she insisted. "I'll have far more fun riding shotgun with you. Besides, I want to know who commissioned Vicky to do the piece as much as you do. Not to mention I'm curious as to what it all means, though I think your colleagues in there will work it out one way or the other even without Vicky's help."

Rob glanced at El. "When's the briefing?" Rob asked.

"It was supposed to be eight tomorrow morning, but we've all but wrapped up the critical aspect of finding the painting," El replied.

"Waldron might try and buy us some time to work out what the hell's going on," Rob added. "The Gallery has to be in an uproar after having most of its frontage and those landmark columns decimated. Last I heard, the street was still closed down, so they can't expect us to hand over the Cezanne immediately."

Sally grinned and cast a laughing look to James.

"I bet we can help with that," she interjected. "Maybe if you pass along word some specialist contractors are doing routine study of it, that might buy you some time. I'd love to get a private viewing of that piece."

"We will all need some rest soon," El continued as if she hadn't heard Sally.

Sally chuckled, knowing full well Rob's partner was teasing, not wanting to spur them on any further into mischief.

"I'm lagging on the tail end of my second wind," El confessed. "With tea, I can write the report, but I'll need to crash for an hour or two on the cots if we're going to be here for too many more shifts without relief."

"I've...uh, managed an hour or so of shut eye," Rob confessed.

Sally looked at the floor to not giggle at this statement.

"How about I start to write the reports when Sally and I get back," Rob offered. "That way I can include whatever we glean from our interview with this Vicky Parker. I owe you that since it was you and James who recovered the painting and all."

"Don't you dare send them out until I've proofed it," El insisted. "I know you'll lay all the glory at James' and my feet and it's no such thing. You worked just as hard with the background work."

"We can argue about it later," Rob said.

Sally stifled a laugh. She'd fallen into that trap too often to count. Rob would change the subject and still go along his merry way doing what he felt was best.

"Just don't leave it till the last minute," Sally warned. "You know what you get like when you leave those mountains of paperwork until they're past due."

Rob groaned. A number of times he'd come over to her flat, a mountain of reports to fill out, and she'd seen him end up still awake in the wee hours of the morning, overdosed on caffeine, jittering at his computer monitor hammering out increasingly incoherent reports because he hadn't kept abreast of the mundane paperwork.

"I'll pick up my leather folder and start jotting notes while Sal drives us to her friend's place," he promised.

"See that you do," El replied. "I'll add in a few addendums for the bits James and I have done, but you promised to write the bulk of the report. I'm holding you to that. Sally here is my witness."

Sally raised her eyebrows at El, a part of her not wanting a piece of that argument, but willingly remaining silent. James wrapped his arm around El's shoulders and they turned to make their way down the corridor and out into the main floor of the office area. Sally threaded her arm through Rob's, feeling sympathy for the poor guy.

"Next time don't let the chivalrous side of your nature get the best of you," she teased him. "You know you loathe the paperwork, why bring more of it onto yourself?"

"Because I suck," he grumbled good-naturedly. "Actually, I was feeling guilty for being asleep, full of happy dreams and sated bliss while El and James were in trouble earlier."

Sally chuckled, but felt curious about what kind of trouble El and James had gotten into earlier. She'd seen El and Rob catching up back in the laboratory. She'd have to get the story out of him, but now wasn't the time.

They wandered down the hall, each lost in their own thoughts. Rob stopped. She looked at him, pleased just to be in his company. When he dipped his head, Sally's heart raced.

Rob stole an all too brief kiss, but it sent her blood pounding nevertheless. Her hands automatically reached up to thread behind his neck, so she could arch her back and press her breasts into the solid warmth of his chest.

She moved her lips over his, as if it were their bodies coming together sexually as they had earlier. Sally opened her mouth and before she could breathe, Rob's tongue was in her, parrying for control. They tasted each other deeply, and Sally moaned, needing him more than her next breath.

"Shhh," Rob murmured into her ear.

Their bodies were still melded together, but she struggled to get oxygen. Sally could hardly believe a simple kiss now had her quivering, a flushed, excited mess of nerve endings and thrumming blood waiting to be taken. She'd have him here, right in the corridor up against the wall, if he'd be bold enough to take her.

A door slammed around the corner somewhere, and reality crashed into her like a bucket of cold water. They separated and Sally fanned her face, trying to cool her color down. A bit more stiffly—she had the feeling Rob was hiding one hell of an erection—they came out into the large, open-planned office.

As they worked their way past Rob's desk, he paused to pick up a fresh pen and a large notepad. He stuck both in his folder. They turned to head for the door and she let him lead the way. Her brain was still fuzzy and full of sexual chemistry. Rob dipped his hand into the pocket of his trousers and pulled out the keys. He tossed them casually into the air. She marveled he had enough brain power to catch them. Sally knew she certainly couldn't have with the way her body hummed with need.

Determined to prove her mind was now on the task at hand, she took the keys from him. The metal clinked together. They exchanged smiles and when they reached the two elevators, Sally pressed the call button. The comfortable silence didn't need to be broken as they each thought their own things. When they entered the lift, Rob activated the signal to take them to the private, underground car park. Sally linked her arm warmly through his and rested her head against him. She enjoyed his faint scent, the strength of his body under her touch a pleasant distraction.

The elevator moved down.

Chapter Four

"Is there a way to keep Vicky out of this?" Sally asked as she drove the car.

Rob had been scrawling and muttering for the last few minutes. When Sally'd overheard him say something about '...*precursor to the bloody report I'm doomed to spend hours...*' she'd decided a change in topic was due. She glanced down at his notebook and his usually difficult to decipher writing had become all but illegible.

He might be annoyed at the interruption now, she thought, but he'd thank her later. Clearly he was getting worked up over something, likely the case and the mountain of paperwork it would generate. She knew how much he hated reports and the more administrative side of his job. Besides, if his writing got even more illegible he'd become further frustrated at two in the morning when he couldn't read what he'd written. A brief distraction now might help him calm down and focus better.

Sally looked away from the road and caught her lover's gaze. His mind seemed to tick over and he caught up to where her question was. She returned her gaze back to where they were going. They were nearly at Vicky's and she wanted to pay attention, find a good parking spot.

Silence filled the car, but she could hear the weight of his thoughts. She bit down lightly on her lower lip and furrowed her brow slightly. Scanning the curb, she couldn't see anything free down this street. She cast a swift glance at Rob, wondering if he'd gone back to his report. She jolted in surprise when she caught him staring at her, a twinkle in his dark eyes.

"What?" she queried. Lifting a hand to rub at her nose, she wondered if she'd had paint or something smeared there this whole time. Rob grinned at her warmly and she moved her attention back to her driving.

"Nothing. You're just adorable. You make my breath catch. I can't believe how lucky I am."

She grinned.

"Too right you're lucky. I know El is a brilliant partner for these missions of yours, but today I'm your lucky charm. Vicky can hopefully give us the answers you need and is the missing key to this thing."

Out of her peripheral vision she saw Rob shake his head. She lightly tapped the brakes and turned the corner. She continued cruising slowly, looking for a spot.

"Sal, you're perfect and I can't wait to prove that to you, now and every day in the future. As to your question earlier, unless your friend knowingly took part in a crime, or willingly acted as an accomplice or co-conspirator, she has nothing to worry about. Even if she falls somewhere in the gray area, I doubt the Agency will want to cause problems for her. You realize we don't beat people with rubber hoses or torture them for being human, right?"

"That's not what I'm worried about," she said. She had no illusions about Bobby. He was a moral, upright man who strongly believed in justice and the right thing. She had no doubts he made life miserable in many ways for bad people. He'd likely even done his share of violence in the past and would do so if called for again in the future. But 'beating people with a rubber hose' just was not his style. Not ever. The thought of it made her want to chuckle.

"It's just...well, Vicky might have a somewhat checkered past," she tried to clarify. While Sally also considered herself an inherently moral person, she knew some of her beliefs weren't as black and white as Rob's. She saw more shades of gray and had room in her belief system for taking other factors into account. And a number of her acquaintances had less white and more gray shades in *their* personal codes.

She didn't want to put Rob on the spot, nor get any of her friends into trouble.

The moment of silence stretched out and she focused fully on looking for a parking space. She could hear Rob thinking again, and cast a glance at him. His jaw and body were relaxed. He smiled. Feeling relieved, she waited for him to marshal his thoughts.

"Let me make a few deductions here, love," he started.

Sally relaxed. His tone was light and comforting. She knew then and there that this wasn't going to be an issue.

"Victoria Parker is outwardly a restorer—paintings predominantly—and probably only known of in certain circles of the art world," Rob guessed, very accurately. "While she'll never work on a truly famous piece, she's talented and solidly mid-range. In other sections—the more shadowed and quieter ones, I'm betting—she's privately a bit of a forger, but only for select people whom she knows and trusts. She's very low key and not remotely interested in anything overtly illegal. Only the shady, possibly even borderline criminal stuff. Nothing heavy or hard core. She's a dabbler and in general a good person. Probably very nice and quite friendly. How am I doing?"

"You're far too intelligent to ask such a stupid question when you know very well the answer already." Sally sniffed disdainfully. She was secretly relieved Rob understood the situation so perfectly. She just didn't want to pander to his ego any more than she already had. In many ways, Sally knew she worshiped Rob—he was a brilliant, wonderful man. He didn't have an over-enlarged ego, or unearned arrogance, but neither was she going to gush over him like some virginal school girl with a crush.

Rob chuckled and she could feel his gaze riveted on her. She stared out of the windscreen, her chin tilted, refusing to look at him.

She didn't need to read his mind to know he understood he'd hit it perfectly on every score in relation to Vicky.

"So we can assume a few things," Rob continued jovially. "One, since you are certain the work would take time, it was done a while ago, possibly before the Gallery even had possession of the painting. Two, Vicky will know who gave her the piece to restore. And from that, we can take a leap of faith and hope that, three, that same person organized for the codes to be made in the painting."

"Will you need Vicky to make a statement, go on record or testify—whatever it is that usually happens?" Sally asked, turning worried eyes upon him again.

Rob hissed.

Sally's attention snapped back to the road and she swerved the car. She'd gotten a little too close to the rear bumper of the car in front of them. About to defer the conversation, she suddenly found an empty spot.

"Ah ha!" she crowed. Feeling a righteous thrill from success in finding a parking place in the city she twisted the wheel sharply. She swerved the car into the tiny spot, parking in a fluid, graceful motion.

Switching off the ignition, Sally then turned in her seat. She beamed proudly at Rob and saw he'd lost a bit of color. True, she might have been a bit over-vigorous in taking her spot, but had she hesitated even a moment, some other vulture would have snatched it from her.

"Bloody hell, now I remember why I never let you drive, Sal. I can't make promises when it comes to the crunch, that's up to Waldron, not me," he said. "I can say that I doubt it will come to that. Vicky is a small piece of the larger puzzle. If she only restored the painting, covering over the invisible additions someone made, she had no knowledge of what she was really doing. We're really just tying up the loose ends anyway. With luck we can crack the code and have far bigger fish to fry here. In the end, it's the person who had this added we want, not Vicky."

"I guess it's too much to ask to not have her name in that report?" Sally said as they both removed their seat belts. She felt a bit sad, already knowing the answer, but needed to ask it anyway. Rob twisted his mouth in a frown.

"I'm sorry, Sal. All I can promise is that I'll do what I can to protect her, but I truly don't think Waldron will see her as more than a link in the chain leading to those responsible."

She nodded and sent him a small smile. Rob reached out, stroked the backs of his fingers down her cheek. She tilted her head, leaning into the light caress, loving the fact she didn't have to hide her true feelings anymore. Better than that, she knew Bobby was hers, heart and soul, just as she was his. Having him in her life so much deeper, more intimately now was like a dream come true, like one of her magical paintings coming to life. She couldn't wait to explore their new life, together, forever.

Shaking her head, she took a deep breath. Not only wasn't this solving Rob's puzzle, but she didn't want him distracted at work like this. She needed to remind herself this was his deal, and she was just along to help and enjoy the ride. Sally hated the thought of putting him on the spot or making his work more difficult than it really was.

"I know I'm making a big deal of this, making your job harder," she apologized. "I'm sorry, Bobby. It's not like she's my best friend. She's not you, whom I'd do anything to protect. But that doesn't mean I want to expose her to possible criminal charges and a whole lot of legal trouble, either."

"I'll word myself carefully in the report," he promised.

Her gaze rested upon him. She trusted him implicitly. He was a good man, the very best. She knew he'd do exactly as he said.

"There," Rob said. "I've just doubled the amount of time I'll need to write that bloody thing. Be grateful I'm not forcing you to critique it before I pass it over to

El. Chances are I'd need to wake you at two in the morning to do so."

"Since I'm the one responsible for your hardship now, I reckon I can spend the night at your place tonight, be on hand for when you finish it at some horrid hour. How does that sound?"

"Mmm," Rob murmured.

He leaned close, kissed her hungrily. Passion raged through her. She could so easily lose herself in this large, solid man. He was truly her knight in shining armor. Big and strong, moral and straight as an arrow, he was like a beacon drawing her into the light of his inherent goodness.

She wanted him badly. Sally longed to feel his hands on her skin, to lick and touch his every inch. She didn't care that they were in the car, out in the middle of a street, she wanted him inside her, over her, surrounding her. Every glance they shared, the tilt of his head, the easy way he smiled at her, even the way he thrust his chin out when he was being stubborn, everything about him drove her crazy with desire.

Sally knew without a doubt she'd never grow tired or get over him. She couldn't imaging a time or place she'd not feel the urge to taste him or have those warm, enormous arms wrap themselves around her, be her safe harbor and keep her from harm.

She adored him. And from the heated intensity of his gaze, she knew he felt very similar to her. Right now, Bobby looked like he could lick her clean and eat her whole. Usually in total, icy control of himself and his emotions, this was the secret, passionate, scorching hot side to Bobby she felt lucky to witness.

Her heart overflowed with love for this man.

"I love it when you look at me like that," Sally confessed. "Your dark gaze just burns into me, as if you can see all my secrets and yet you're still hungry for more."

"I wish I could," he murmured, kissing her again. "I love you, Sal. Every inch of you, for good or bad. Most especially I adore your enormous heart, your zest for life. You're the most precious thing in my world. You know that, right?"

"I have an inkling," she said.

Rob ran his fingers through her hair, spiking her hair in disarray. She batted at his hands, the tiny, rational part of her brain not wanting to look too bed-tousled when they finally got out of the car. Unable to help herself, she wrapped her arms around his neck and kissed him passionately instead. Rob moaned and drew her close to his body.

Laughing, breathless, she pulled away. Her heart hammered a hard tattoo. Knowing now that the acrobatic and somewhat uncomfortable sport of car sex was truly on the table, Sally decided she needed to pretend to be the mature adult for once. She unlocked her door and opened it a crack.

"We're on a mission," she reminded him. "We should at least pretend to be professional."

"Absolutely, madam," Rob teased her.

She threw him a naughty look then climbed out of the car. Her heart skipped happily, lighter than she could ever recall before. Her world was perfect. She had her painting, she was helping on an important case and she had her love and personal hero, Bobby, right here by her side, in her bed and always in her life. Nothing could possibly get better than this.

Rob met her on the sidewalk and beeped the car locked. Sally took his hand in hers, twined their fingers together and set off down the street, leading them to her friend's house.

* * * *

Victoria Parker was not anything like he'd thought. Rob rarely let himself have preconceived notions — far too often they would make him overlook something while he searched for what he expected. He'd learned ages ago to keep an open mind and observe everything, making his deductions and analyzing what was truly there and not what he thought or wanted things to be.

While he had not consciously made perceptions about Vicky, the five foot two, extremely cuddly, middle-aged woman who answered the door was not even close. Her pale blonde hair was professionally cut into a wispy cap around her head and her blue eyes sparkled with barely suppressed humor as she opened the door.

"Sally, what a pleasant surprise. I wasn't expecting you, dear, was I?"

Rob found himself tilting to the side, peering into the house and looking for Victoria, half of the opinion this woman couldn't possibly be the shady restorer and forger he searched for.

"No, Vicky, this is rather a sudden stop. This is Rob. Can we come in, please?"

Sally's words snapped him back to attention, embarrassed he could be so careless as to not see what was before his very eyes. "Of course," the blonde fluttered, clearly baffled but happy and seemingly used to that state of mind.

"Madam." Rob nodded in polite greeting as he entered after Sally. He found himself slouching. More than a foot taller than Vicky, he didn't want her to feel crowded or loomed over.

"Please, both of you, sit. Can I get you some tea? Maybe some toast or a light snack?" Vicky waved a hand toward the couch and the two brightly patterned chairs that flanked it.

The parlor was filled with framed paintings taking up most of the three walls. A grandfather clock ticked in the corner and a large set of bay windows looked out onto the street, sheer curtains protecting their privacy. The chair nearest the electric heater had a small table set up next to it, a basket of embroidery, a stack of paperback novels and small sketch pad all vying for space. The notebook was well used, the earlier pages dog-eared and some creased, though they were turned over so a fresh sheet was ready with a few pencils, presumably for when inspiration struck.

That chair clearly was her usual spot, closest to the heater and turned so she could easily glance out of the large windows onto the street when it suited her.

"I'm fine thanks," Sally replied as she glanced to Rob.

He shook his head. "Nothing for me, thank you," he murmured. He placed his leather folder on the small table to one side.

Sally had already taken a seat on the couch and so he sat next to her, leaving her regular chair clear for Vicky.

Vicky perched on the edge of the cushion, clasped her hands together and seemed to gather her courage. "Am I in trouble?" Vicky asked bluntly.

Rob tried to shift back on the couch, letting Sally take the lead but also to make himself appear less threatening. The over-stuffed cushions seemed to suck him in deeper. He wasn't sure he'd be able to extract himself with a crowbar when the time came for them to leave.

"Oh, no," Sally rushed to reassure her friend. "Not at all. Actually Rob and I are here to ask for your help. I recognized your work, a touch up of a Cezanne you must have done a few years ago. It was in the National Gallery."

"Hmm. Yes, I remember that piece. It was genuine, or I certainly believe so. I only needed to work on a few areas, nothing too taxing at all." Vicky's shoulders visibly relaxed. She seemed to realize they weren't they there to drag her in to jail in chains. "I touched up the sky and some of the background, I believe. I remember I had awful trouble trying to get the various greens of the grass just right. Even though it was a small section, it took me most of a week to complete. Is there a problem?"

"Not to do with you or your restoration," Sally insisted. "But we need to know who hired you to undertake the work. It's terribly important, I promise, or we wouldn't be here."

At that moment, Rob glanced outside the window. A tall, lanky man walked past for the second time. Rob's instincts stirred. This was a fairly quiet street. Only three cars had passed in the last ten minutes. Dusk was gathering, but there was still plenty of brightness left in the sky—the street lights hadn't turned themselves on yet. In fifteen or twenty minutes, though, when Rob gauged he and Sally would be leaving, it would be properly twilight, near dark.

Years of training kept him aware of his surroundings and thinking ahead. He loathed the word paranoid, but with Sally accompanying him, he was naturally inclined to be over-cautious. Frowning thoughtfully, he became more alert and watched for that lanky man. Positive they hadn't been followed, he wondered if he should have scanned his vehicle before leaving the office. Their enemies wouldn't need to tail them if there was a tracking device on his bloody car.

Rob cursed himself for not thinking about it earlier.

Definitely falling into paranoid city, my man, he chided himself. *The poor sod is probably lost or circling the block on his daily constitutional. No need to go off the deep end just yet.*

Despite his mental pep talk, Rob wished he were handier with a gun. Back at HQ he'd surreptitiously slipped a tiny clutch piece — a .25 caliber side arm El had bullied him into practicing with — into his leather folder from his desk drawer. El was the shooter in their partnership. Not only was she far more accurate with the weapon than he, but she was easily the more comfortable with it, too.

Rob preferred to think or talk his way out of problems. Of course there were exceptions and he reluctantly practiced with his small piece for those times when he faced someone who was more inclined to shoot first and speak after. That was not a common problem he faced, though.

"…I'm truly sorry, Sally."

Rob had only been listening to the conversation with half an ear. When Sally nudged him discreetly, he shifted his focus away from the window and street outside and more fully on the women.

"I understand you're not comfortable divulging your sources, madam," Rob said without missing a beat in the conversation. "But this isn't an idle inquiry from curiosity or nosiness. That piece was crucial in the attack on the Gallery the other day. I'm working for a firm investigating those responsible and it's come to our attention this particular piece has been altered sometime in the past. Not your work, let me assure you, but other information has been added with great care. It's vital we track down those who did this and work out its importance."

"Oh." Vicky managed to look both mollified and intrigued. "Well, I might be able to contact them, pass along your details and request they contact you. I'm sure you can understand in such a small industry as mine, privacy and one's reputation can be the difference between getting work and starving."

"Of course," Rob said soothingly. "Would it make a difference if I left the room? You could discuss matters privately with Sally—who I know is a friend of yours. It might be easier for you as she isn't associated with more official lines, like myself?"

"Well I...I wouldn't want you to think... I mean..." Vicky clearly floundered.

Rob smiled gently as he worked his way out of the clutches of the sofa.

He stood and turned to pick up his things, but his eye was caught once again by that same man walking out front of the house.

Once he barely registered. Twice and it was noticeable. Three times and a warning sounded in his brain.

"Miss Parker"—Rob turned sideways to point at the man down the street as he waved at someone and rounded the corner—"is that a neighbor of yours, perhaps? It's the third time I've—"

The sound of tires squealing on the asphalt outside cut his words off. It only took three of his long strides to cross the room, twitch the sheer curtain to the side and peer out. A low slung, new model black saloon had turned onto the street, going so fast around the bend it was practically on two wheels. Rob saw both the front and back windows scroll down—all the glass in the car heavily tinted like in some B grade gangster movie.

"Sal! Vicky! Get down, now!" he roared, but most of his words were cut off by the metallic, rapid shot fire of automatic weapons. Rob leaped across the room, his instincts screaming to protect the women. In the back of his mind though, all was calm and still. Thoughts ticked by in quick snaps, his brain clear despite the panic that simmered under the surface.

Away from the window. We'll be protected by the wall. Maybe behind the furniture.

His mind rapped out thoughts and directions, the loud staccato of the gunfire receding into the background as his whole intent focused on getting Sally and Vicky to safety.

It was only as he barreled across the room, his arms spread, his body moving forward in a classic tackle pose, that he registered the bullets were coming through the walls. The windows shattered, glass spraying everywhere and raining down over him, but he'd expected that the instant he'd heard the snap of bullets.

But if the projectiles made it through the front facade of the house itself, they were armor piercing rounds and far more deadly than he'd expected.

"Down!" he bellowed.

Debris flew everywhere and Rob was forced to hunch his shoulders and duck his head to protect his face. He hauled Sally up from the couch, using his much larger body as a shield between her and the bullets. Easily lifting her weight with one arm, Rob knew that adrenaline lent him far more strength than he usually had. Rob grabbed Vicky and dragged her with him behind the couch. He groaned as a searing pain burned across his arm. The fire had nothing to do with lifting Vicky. It was a different agony all together.

Rob cast a fleeting glance at his arm, not surprised in the least to see blood staining his shirt dark red and spreading quickly.

"Son of a bitch," he said.

Hurling both women together down onto the floor, delicacy be damned, he quickly followed them. Without a single thought, he covered their bodies with his.

The entire attack could barely have lasted more than thirty seconds.

It felt like a lifetime.

An eerie stillness filled the air as the bullets stopped. Rob strained his ears, praying the occupants of the car wouldn't come in to finish the job. His sodding gun was still on the table by the couch, safely stowed away and far out of reach. It could have been on the moon for all the good it would do him right now.

The car engine revved, tires squealed for the second time and they peeled away.

Both women gasped for breath beneath him, but Rob waited a few more seconds, listening intently to be certain the coast was clear. More than one agent in the past had been shot by a lingering enemy, waiting for their prey to think they were safe and stick their head out to survey the damage.

No one knew he and Sally were here. They hadn't filed a report, hadn't checked with anyone. This had to be a hit on Vicky. Someone, it appeared, was tying up loose ends. He needed to get Vicky and Sally safely stowed away and before a crowd gathered to notice them and comment on the strange visitors who were with Victoria Parker when her house was shot up to shit.

Heart hammering, he knelt onto his knees, remaining behind the couch still but removing his weight from the ladies.

"Sal, Vicky, I need you both to be ready to run the instant I say so."

He reached out around the side of the couch so he could grab his folder and jerk it to him, cursing again as papers fell out of it and scattered everywhere on the floor. Digging his gun out with one hand, Rob shoved what papers he could back in with his other. Wincing as the papers were crumpled and crushed, he decided that speed was more important than keeping the documents pristine. He gathered everything he could manage in a few short seconds then zipped it up. Shoving it under his free arm, he tried to assess the situation as calmly as he could manage.

"Right," he panted.

His arm was painfully raw and sweat beaded his brow, but he had bigger problems to deal with. Feeling optimistic — no one had entered the decimated house — he hoped their attackers had all left in the car. He'd recognize the man from the street, and with his arm turning to agony now, Rob knew he'd not resist shooting if he needed to.

"Sal, Vicky…what, what's happened?"

Rob's focus changed from planning escape to panic.

Sally sobbed as she leaned over Vicky, the woman struggling to speak.

"It's okay, it's okay," Sally repeated.

Vicky clearly was agitated, trying to move and lifting her head up. She remained splayed on the floor where he'd left her, her neck and chest saturated with dark red.

Sally's hands were covered in blood, the viscous fluid sticking to her jeans, her shirt and smeared over her skin as she struggled to stem the flow seeping from Vicky's neck wound.

"Shit. Shit," he said. Dropping his folder to the floor, he placed the gun in reach nearby. He knelt down and lifted Sally's hands.

"Sally, are you hit?" he snapped out, wincing as more blood bubbled out of Vicky. Since his shirt was already ripped, he tore off the bottom half of his sleeve, rolled it into a tightly packed ball and pressed it to Vicky's neck, exerting as much pressure as he dared.

In seconds the cloth had soaked through, and he knew something serious had been hit. There was far too much blood in too short a time.

"Sally," Vicky panted.

Sally leaned closer, took her friend's hand. Feeling helpless, Rob did what he could, knowing in his heart it would be of no use.

"It's okay, Vicky," Sally sobbed. "I'll tell them. It's going to be okay."

Vicky sighed and Rob felt the life leave her. Sally cried harder. Rob was torn. It was wretched, but he couldn't give Sally more than a few moments to grieve her friend. Brushing his fingers lightly over Vicky's eyes—though he knew she was well beyond pain now—he closed her lids. With a deep breath, Rob leaned back on his feet. He tried to calm his heart rate and panting. Sally struggled valiantly, clearly trying to get herself back under control.

He wrapped an arm around her shoulders, hugging her tightly, willing his warmth to seep into her body.

"She told me..." Sally gasped, unable to speak properly. "She was lying there, dying, and she told me the name."

"We need to move, Sal," he said as gently as possible. "We can't have anyone knowing we were here. I think someone ordered Vicky's death, hired professionals. Sal, love, if they have even an inkling she told you, they'll come after us next. I won't risk your safety."

"But the police—"

"Are obliged to file reports, detain witnesses. You'll be a sitting duck. I can protect you. Sal, do you trust me?"

Sally lifted her face. His heart wrenched. Her eyes were enormous, her cheeks streaked from tears. She was worryingly pale and clearly distraught. She lifted a hand to wipe her nose, but her gaze widened as she caught sight of her blood-stained skin. A horrified look crossed her face.

Harsh as he knew it would seem, Rob forced himself to act. He desperately wanted to wrap Sally safely in his arms, cradle her to his body and rock her, kiss away the pain and shock and make everything better. But there wasn't time. Already he could hear the sirens getting louder. Rob would bet the local precinct's switchboard had lit up within seconds of the first shot being fired. Vicky's home would be inundated in minutes, if not sooner. Their window of opportunity to escape was closing.

Rob gave her his handkerchief, but then immediately took Sally's free hand in his. Lowering their linked fingers out of her range of vision—so she couldn't continue to stare, captivated, by Vicky's blood—he tugged Sal to her feet while she wiped her nose.

Bending down, he picked up his folder and held it out to Sally. She put away the stained cloth then took his folder. None of these actions seemed to register in her eyes or any other sense. She was on automatic pilot, he guessed, her mind numbing as it tried to adjust to everything.

He loathed himself for bringing her into this and hoped she could forgive him one day. It would kill him if that innocence he cherished in her had been shattered. He would grieve if he never saw that look of wonder, just from the joy she found in the world, on her face again.

Picking up his gun and holding it low beside his body, Rob surveyed the ruined room and narrowed in on the corridor leading toward the back of the house.

"Come on, Sal," he said, more to hear the words aloud and not the unnaturally still quiet. "It's going to be all right. I'll take care of you. We're going to fix this somehow, I promise."

"I'm okay," she said, though her tone sounded dull.

Rob cast a look at her as he led her through the house out to the kitchen area. The room was cozy, another large set of windows that in the summer would let the sun in. He bet it would be a perfect breakfast nook, warm and intimate.

Better still, there was a back door leading out into a small garden.

"Let's go," he said, more for the sake of talking than actually asking her permission.

She didn't resist as he led her through the kitchen. The key sat in the lock. He turned it, then opened the door. He let go of Sally's hand for a moment to step out and check there was no one in the vicinity.

All the action appeared to be occurring on the street out front. Rob tightened his hand around the gun, his heart beating fast from the unsteady mixture of nerves and adrenaline. He hated the thought of innocent civilians crowding around and despised the necessity for the gun, but if those men attacked again, he needed to be ready. Not just to protect himself and Sal, but possibly all those potential hostages now wondering what had just occurred.

"Coast's clear."

He stepped back, took Sally's hand again, not bothered by the drying, rust-colored blood that now stained them both. Sally looked like she'd bathed in it, though his arm was just as bad and hurt like a bitch. Scanning the area, he saw a small gate near the back of the property.

Rob led Sally, still silent and unresisting, to it, then pressed her hand lightly. The fence was only slightly higher than he was, so when he stood on his toes, he could see over the top. A quick survey showed no one he could see.

"I'm grateful we had to park a few streets away," he said, trying to be upbeat. He hated the thought of what a cabbie would say should they try to flag a taxi just now. And even though the tube saw all manner of strange sights every day, two blood-stained people sitting mildly at the station would surely attract more attention than they wanted.

"Here's hoping we don't get called in for trespassing, eh?" he added as he closed the gate behind them, took Sally's hand again and squeezed it.

Her eyes flickered and she seemed to focus on him properly for the first time since the gun shots had started.

"I don't want to go back to your office," she stated, some of her strength returning.

Rob released her hand, wrapped his arm around her shoulder and drew her close against his body. Kissing her forehead, he enjoyed that one second of time where it was just the two of them. He then led them toward the street that ran behind Vicky's home and tried to orient himself as to where they'd parked.

"We'll go back to my place," he said, making sure to keep only warmth in his tone. "You'll feel better after you've cleaned up."

"Do you need a hospital?" she asked.

"Nah," Rob insisted, surprised. Clearly Sally's brain was starting to once again take in her surroundings. "This is just a scratch. I have some bandages and adhesive tape at home that we can use to protect and close the wound."

Sally wrapped her arm around his waist, leaned her head against him and they slowly made their way back to the car. Rob knew she was a far cry from feeling perfect, but there was color in her cheeks and much of her usual calm was returning. He'd know in the next few hours, but he hoped he hadn't caused her irreparable damage.

Holding her like the precious object she was to him, Rob returned to the car and tried to puzzle out what the hell was going on.

Chapter Five

Rob had purposely kept his bathroom door open to keep an ear out for Sally while he made a couple of quick calls. Firstly he'd called Waldron, letting him know they'd need a few agents for containment at Vicky's place. Word would trickle through London slowly, but sooner or later there would be connections between a recent art heist and the very visible murder of an art restorer. It might even be a day or two, but someone would put those pieces together at some stage. The Agency needed to be ready to field questions when they did.

Waldron appreciated the heads up, and despite complaining of another ruined evening and potentially long night appeasing the various political powers that be, he seemed resigned to remaining at HQ for the foreseeable future.

Rob's second call had been somewhat longer, and more delicate.

"Williams."

"El, it's Rob. Look, I have some bad news."

"If you've thought of some lame arse excuse to try and shove the writing of that bloody report onto me, you can stick it in the orifice of your choice. I'm hoping to drag James away from here sometime in the next hour or so, grab some take-out and then sleep for a solid eight hours."

"No," Rob sighed, then thought of his folder spewing papers in the gunfight. He'd grabbed what he could, but had no idea whether he'd gotten it all. It was possible he'd lost the notes he'd made. "Though I think I might have lost what little of the rough draft I'd managed to scrawl up, I'll have to check my folder later. Look, we were attacked at Vicky Parker's place—"

"Hold on. Attacked? Where are you?"

Rob heard James swear in the background.

"James? Rob? What the fuck? One of you, tell me what's going on."

"Sally is friends with Vicky Parker, the restorer—or forger depending on your viewpoint—who touched up the Cezanne after someone added those codes. We went to question her. A group of people, at least four of them, shot up the house, armor piercing rounds, can you believe? Vicky was critically hit in the neck. She bled out in less than a minute. Sal and I tried to save her, but it was impossible."

"Oh, shit. How is Sally? Are either of you hurt?"

"We've got some scrapes, a few scratches and bruises. I've let Waldron know, but it's a bloody mess right now. Sal is pretty upset. She's in the shower, I think. Look...keep an eye on James. We'll come in soon, but I need to make sure Sal is okay before I take her back to HQ. I'm still on board for the report, but it just got a whole lot more complicated. I believe Vicky managed to tell Sally who hired her, but this isn't the time for me to push her."

"Don't worry about any of that, I'll cover things from here. Take care of Sally," El reassured him.

Rob heaved a sigh of relief, pleased to have El say that. It took a load from his mind.

"I owe you, El," he thanked her.

She huffed out a laugh. "I know, and you're going to pay me back by still writing this report. Look, if you need anything, either of you, call me. Okay?"

"I promise. I need to go to her. Talk later, El."

After saying their goodbyes, he closed his phone, took a deep breath and stripped out of his bloodstained shirt and pants. In only his boxers, he entered the bathroom, surprised and saddened to see Sal sitting on the tiled floor underneath the warm spray, still fully dressed. Her knees raised as she pulled her arms around them, she huddled in the corner, her head lowered and her nose red. She'd evidently been crying.

Rob silently pulled two enormous, fluffy, fresh towels from under the sink. He placed them on the edge of the basin then stepped out of his boxers. The air was cool on his naked skin. Rob opened the door to the shower stall then closed it behind him. The water pounded on him, drenching him in seconds. He crouched down then sat next to Sally.

She turned immediately to face him. He wrapped an arm strongly around her, hugging her to his side. Pressing a kiss to her forehead, he then tenderly brushed her soaking hair from her eyes.

"I thought she might have to answer questions from the police," Sally said huskily. Her voice sounded creaky, as if her throat was raw from crying. "Or maybe they'd have a file on her and want to push her for details on her past jobs, something like that. She never played with the big boys, she was proud of the fact she always took the small, manageable jobs that paid well and helped her make ends meet. Plus she loved the thrill of it, the extra push she felt to stretch her talents. If I'd had even an inkling we'd bring those people to her door—"

"Hey," he cut her off. He kept his voice low and soft but the tone firm so she couldn't ignore him. "Sal. Listen to me. Carefully, okay?"

He waited till she nodded, a jerky motion.

"Sal, we didn't bring this to her door. I swear it. I might have looked distracted, and you're a very strong temptation to me, but I checked our tail thoroughly. Call it my latent paranoia, courtesy of working at the Agency coupled with that slightly non-linear method of thinking we talked about earlier today. We weren't followed, and there's not a chance we were tapped or listened to inside HQ. That's not possible. I promise."

Sally shivered but remained silent. For a moment he thought she might not believe him, or wasn't listening. His heart stung. He tried to reword himself mentally, get his point across in a stronger way. He'd tell her over and over until she believed him if that's what she needed.

"It wasn't us?" she said quietly. Sally lifted her head, blinked the water from her eyes as she tried to meet his gaze.

Rob brushed his fingers lightly over her face, waited until she'd locked eyes with him. "It wasn't us. I swear. I knew she was your friend, and I made sure we wouldn't bring this to her door. We didn't lead them to her. They were professionals, and they were there to kill her. Bullets don't go through wood and glass like that, not normal ones. They were armor piercing rounds. These guys knew they wanted to attack her and had the right equipment. This wasn't some random drive-by or seizing of an opportunity by following us. They tracked her down and came prepared."

Sally shivered again. She fluttered her eyes shut and nodded. When she looked at him next, her gaze was clearer, sharper.

"Thank you, Bobby. For trying to protect her. I saw how you laid your body over both of us. I know that bullet graze you got was meant for either her or me. You're truly a hero, the most wonderful man."

Rob twisted his mouth wryly. He was about to make a dry comment, but she pressed her fingers to his lips.

"No, don't. You're my guardian. My knight in shining armor. I don't care that you have all that control, or that we've wasted so much time. We're here now and I know the true depths of your feelings. I know you'd do anything to protect those who need it. And though I can't promise I won't worry, I don't even want to be parted from you again. I love you."

"I'm no knight," he insisted. "I was terrified I'd lose you, that you'd be hurt and it would be all my fault. When those shots rang out..." He let the words trail off. His throat constricting just at the memory of that sound, the fear that had inundated him. He'd truly frozen in that moment, unable to breathe or react. It played in his head on repeat, like some horrific movie scene he just couldn't get rid of because it had been real.

A nightmare come to life. Rob shuddered and sighed, hoping he'd be able to scrub the entire scene from his mind from force of will alone. Sally wrapped herself around him, and even though it didn't ease the visions in his head, it was the perfect start.

Sally didn't need to read minds to know that Rob struggled with the danger she'd been in. Even though a part of her wanted to insist she had as much right to be in that room as he, she knew it wasn't that simple. This danger and constant threat of mayhem wasn't her life, wasn't what she was trained for or the world she understood. Add in Rob's fierce desire to protect her, and she knew he'd struggle.

She wanted to help him overcome that, but she also needed him right now for selfish reasons. It was as if her hands were stained with blood, Vicky's life essence. Literally and figuratively she felt dirty, contaminated. But sitting in the shower, hearing the muffled murmur of Rob's voice over the steady flow of water hadn't helped her feel cleansed. Now, in her lover's arms, feeling his warmth and strength, she came alive in a manner she'd never known possible.

It was as if his every touch shined over her skin, as if he were recreating her, bringing her out of the darkness and into his perfect light. The sense was heady and acted more potently than a bottle of wine ever could.

"You're my knight, my hero, and you're perfect. I won't hear otherwise," she insisted, pressing against his body and kissing him with a ferocious hunger. "Damn these wet clothes," she said.

Rob's chuckle echoed in the tiled room. All of a sudden, Sally couldn't bear the wet, weighted press of her clothes against her skin anymore. With far more haste than grace, she began to peel the soaked items from her body. Rob helped her pull the heavy, wet jeans down her legs, but she managed to shed the rest in record time considering the circumstances.

Minutes later she was naked, feeling reborn — or about to be. Bobby was hard as steel and deliciously warm. Her breaths came in short little pants. She was eager, curious and looking forward to the chance to explore him in every intimate, minute detail.

Rob opened the shower door. Sally giggled when the steady stream of water from the shower head sprayed out onto the tiles. As she watched, Rob pulled open the middle drawer of the vanity and grabbed a condom from the packet.

When he closed the door again, steam soon enveloped them. The warmth returned quickly this time, and she eagerly helped him sheath himself. He placed his large arms around her, and Sally had never felt more cherished or safer. Kissing him slowly, she explored his mouth, prying his lips open with her tongue and tasting him.

He parried with her, stroked his hands over her slick flesh, further inflaming the desire building to the inevitable crescendo within her. When she cupped his balls in one hand and fisted his thick cock with the other. He groaned, the sound music to her ears, dripping with passion and need. She'd only previously dreamed of hearing such a moan from him.

"Fuck," he reached out, blindly groped for her. "Love, you need to slow down. I need...we have to...fuck."

Hunger raced through her, blinding her to every instinct that urged her to take her time, relish and treasure every moment. Her legs shook from the intensity of her need. The knot of desire in her stomach twisted, her passion sky rocketed and it was like a fire blazed through her. She wanted him. Right now. Inside her, over her, everywhere.

It felt a little like being possessed by sheer desire and hunger.

"I don't want slow or tender," she insisted. "I need you, Bobby. Right now. Strong. Hot. Fierce. To remind me that we're alive. Please."

Rob pressed her back into the wet tiles of the shower wall. He parted her legs with his thigh and reached a hand low to stroke at her clit. She arched up, shuddering with the sensations buffeting her system. She could no longer think, only feel. When he found her pussy soaked, he groaned again. She was beyond slick.

Needing him urgently, wanting him with her every step here, Sally continued pumping him hard, pushing him closer to the edge. She didn't need lube or assistance, it was clear they were both dangling on the precipice of something magnificent.

"Wait," he panted, his voice sounding strained. "I want to make this good for you. I don't want to rush you."

"You aren't, Bobby," she insisted in a low, almost guttural tone. "I want you to fuck me now. Hard. I'm ready. Please, Bobby. Please, fuck me right now."

She gasped, but his body told her all he couldn't seem to articulate. His hips rocked forward, his cock thrusting into her fist. He fucked her hand as she held him tight. Both their paces increased, became jerky and ragged with need.

For a moment she felt embarrassed. She'd never used such language, or such strong words before. Sally worried he'd be shocked, but conversely the words seem to release some restraint he'd placed upon himself. Her words freed him. The clear need she had gave them both permission to take what they craved. More than that, though, it seemed to bless them, to prove that *fucking* was as acceptable as 'making love'.

"Fuck, you're perfect, Sal," Rob panted. "I'd love to fuck you blind, use you till you come screaming and push us both over the edge and we fall down together into insanity."

Even though she knew the words didn't make a logical kind of sense, they were perfect. Sally knew exactly what Bobby was saying, and it drove her need higher.

"I want us to use each other up, Bobby," she said darkly. "I'll suck every inch of you and expect the same in return. We're destined like that."

He moaned and Sally couldn't articulate what that sound drew from her. He seemed to understand her on a visceral level, as if they'd each taken a peek at the darker fantasies one didn't talk about in polite company. They weren't even something she could put words to, but more images that were branded upon her soul. And she knew Bobby had shadows in him, elemental desires that were never far from the darkness that so frequently clung to him.

She didn't want to banish them, but they could weather it together, share them and be a joint force against them.

It was as if their mutual soul baring had unleashed something intrinsic and elemental inside him. Rob pushed her back into the wall, grabbed her hips and lifted her slightly off the ground. She helped guide his thick, hard cock to the entrance of her pussy. In a long, slow thrust he pressed inside her in one stroke. Sheathed completely, he supported her thighs with his palms, pushing her to wrap her legs around his waist.

"Hold on, Sal," he warned her.

His voice was so thick, so rough, she could barely understand what he said, but the tone and his body told her everything. She tightened her legs around him, urging him on with actions and a guttural groan that seemed torn from her soul. She braced her hands on his shoulders and knew this would be something different, something magical and special.

Rob moved his hips back, lowered his body so his cock withdrew from her heat. In a hard shove, he filled her again swiftly. She cried out, the sound rending through the air. It was a piercing cry, one of possession, submission and both pleasure and pain. He was so thick, so big and even as slick and prepared as she was, she felt utterly possessed. Full to the brim.

She loved it.

Her channel squeezed down on him so tightly she thought she'd pass out from the pleasure. Clenching at him, she caressed him with her inner muscles. He panted harshly, and she knew they were both struggling to breathe, so intense was the moment.

He repeated the motion, fucking her with a hard, determined pace that set her heart racing. This time his shaft was smooth and coated with her juices. His passage was juddery this time and she almost bemoaned the loss of that harder edge. When Bobby shifted his angle, he pressed even deeper inside her and she cried out with bliss.

He fucked her hard and long. Not even in her darkest fantasies had she imagined such mind-blowing pleasure.

Sally moaned, a deep, husky sound that filled the room and reverberated off the tiles. It was like the sound was some sort of siren call. Rob shouted and his actions took on a sense of urgency and near-desperation.

It was as if he released his control, letting her get a glimpse of the hungry, base male beast that resided in his deepest, most private corner. He pounded into her, over and over. When he had a solid rhythm going, he carefully moved one hand around between their bodies to caress her clit. The extra stimulation sent her over the edge. It was like he'd detonated a bomb inside her body. Her stomach tightened, her toes flexed and heat exploded through her every sense.

Her body exploded and she screamed her release, blind, deaf and dumb to everything around her for that shining, perfect moment.

She shook while Rob continued to pound, thrusting his hard cock deeper as her body blossomed open. Her climax released the tense inner muscles and her pussy allowed him to plunge farther. Changing the angle of his hips, he rubbed her G-spot with each plunge and her second orgasm followed hard on the heels of her first.

This time her scream was raw — a shocked sound as he took her completely by surprise. The second climax was far more intense and she'd never experienced one so close to another. Sally gasped for breath, and she dug her fingernails into his shoulder and back. This intimacy seemed to act as a trigger for him. Rob roared his release, shouting hoarsely as he came. His hips snapped forward over and over. He emptied himself into her body. His gestures slowed as he ran out of steam. Panting now, she could feel the tremors of release and aftershocks shake through his body. Rob pressed her back into the wall.

Water cascaded down and around them, washing them both clean. Sally gazed at her lover, smiling at him. The moment wasn't awkward or strange, even though they'd both bared more than their skin to one another. While a part of her wanted to murmur how good it was, a larger part just wanted to enjoy the perfection of this moment exactly as it was.

Enjoying the silence, she lifted her head and kissed him tenderly. He tightened his arms around her, as if he wanted to absorb her into his very body. She clung to him, meeting her lips eagerly with his.

Minutes later, he lifted his head and pulled his cock from her body. He grabbed the washcloth and handed it to her before he discarded the condom.

"If I wasn't so exhausted I'd be looking forwards to seconds," Sally teased.

He chuckled as he turned back. "It might take me a while to recover from that," he admitted. "I'm running out of steam, mentally as well as physically."

Sally ran the cloth over his skin and his eyes fluttered closed. She enjoyed washing him, doing a tiny service after all he'd done for her.

"I've got that bloody report, and I want to take you back to the office. It's safe there."

"They didn't see us, did they?"

Rob shook his head. "No, I don't believe so. We were careful leaving. They took an awful chance, shooting up the front of the house like that. They must have known Vicky tended to sit in that particular chair. The heist of the painting itself was well planned, perfectly executed. This reeks of desperation."

"I totally forgot. Do you know who Erik Chambers is?"

"The name rings a bell, but I don't immediately recognize the person. Should I know him? My brain is fried."

Sally remained silent. He turned, ducked his head beneath the spray and rubbed his hands over his face. She worried for a moment that he was too tired, that it could put him in danger. Rob was a big boy, though, he knew his limits better than she and she didn't want to nag him, or worse, smother him.

He took the cloth from her, rubbed some soap into it and began to carefully, slowly stroke over her skin and clean her. She smiled, enjoying the ministration but not able to conceal her concern for him.

"I know you can't take it, but you need some rest, Bobby."

He opened his mouth, about to insist otherwise and she lifted her hand, placating.

"I know, I've said my piece," she added. "I'll leave it now. As for Erik Chambers, I've heard he's a very kind man. He's a patron of many sculptors and has a keen eye for artwork. He's a collector in the old sense, funding opening showings and offering a helping hand to newer, usually less popular, styles of artists. He's been a hermit for years, though, reclusive to an extreme."

"Rich?" Rob guessed.

Sally nodded and wiped water from her eyes. He rinsed the cloth out once more then hung it up over the back of the showerhead.

"Filthy," she said. "I can't picture him being a part of this. He's helped hundreds of people over the years and donated possibly millions of pounds worth of artwork to the various museums and galleries. He's an entrepreneur, not a criminal."

"Being one doesn't preclude the other," Rob reminded her. He turned off the water faucets. Steam billowed in the cool air. He opened the door and climbed out of the stall. He grabbed a towel then handed it to Sally. After gathering the second for himself, he wrapped it around his waist. He turned to study her.

When he stroked the back of his fingers down her cheek, she shivered. The weight of his glance sent tendrils of lust and need unfurling in her stomach. This time, however, Rob seemed to be studying her quite critically. She realized she must not just look a mess, but probably also as overtired as he, and maybe still a little shocked to boot. It had been an eventful day.

"I'll be okay," she reassured him in a soft tone. "It was an awful lot to take in at once, and I'll be honest, I was terrified to think a normal house had been so brazenly attacked. I kept thinking what would have happened if children had been walking home at the time, or there'd been kids in the street. It's just so far out of the scope of my usual reality I couldn't assimilate it. And the way you threw yourself on us, protected us with your body... Bobby, it made my heart stop with fear for you. You're so brave, unthinkingly so. It stole my breath and I needed some time to wrap my head around it."

"It wasn't brave, it was instinct," he insisted as he dried himself.

Sally pulled the towel around her body, under her arms, and tried to soak up the warmth from the fluffy cotton.

Rob placed his towel around her shoulders, adding another layer against her skin. She cast him a grateful look.

"I'll go search out something that will hopefully not look too ridiculous on you," he said a little gruffly.

"I'm not going back to my loft?" she called out after him when he left the bathroom. She saw Rob walk into his bedroom. She quickly dried her feet and legs, ran the towel over her body and wrapped herself up again. When she entered his bedroom he'd pulled out a long-sleeved cotton shirt that looked a bit mangled and likely shrunk in a bad wash. Touched, she liked the thought of wearing his shirt. It would still be enormous on her, but she couldn't wait to smell his scent all over her.

She didn't like his chances of ever getting the item of clothing back again. Ever.

"Nope," he answered her earlier question. "We're going back to the office. I doubt there's any risk to you," he said. He tossed a pair of shorts that would be almost three-quarter-length pants on her. "But after the last few days, I refuse to risk it. Consider me in full-blown paranoia mode. I want to update El and go see this Erik Chambers. I'm determined to get to the bottom of this. It will also be good to check up with Masters, the analyst Ben mentioned he'd give that code to. I want to see if he's managed to break anything yet. Any extra information we get will be useful."

"So I get to sit and wait?" Sally asked. While most other women, making the same statement, would be bitter or complaining, she was more thoughtful. This really wasn't her career or something she had any real understanding about. Part of her wanted to insist she see it through, but another understood her personal limitation. As exhausted as they all were, she refused to become a liability.

She'd never forgive herself if she turned into one of those stubborn, illogical creatures. It was likely she'd cause Bobby to be distracted and he didn't need that right now. Should he be hurt, or their case compromised because he was busy looking out for her instead of paying attention to the situation...she wasn't sure she could live with that.

"There should be a half-used sketch book here from some of your previous visits that you can use to keep your mind busy, if that's what you're worried about," Rob said. "Besides, there are always Agents coming in and out at odd hours at the office. While I agree it won't be like a busy tube station, there will be people around to speak to and be near. You won't be alone."

Sally smiled at him, touched but also amused. Rob was looking at her, clearly trying to judge how badly shaken she was.

"You don't have to worry about me," she insisted. "I'm not going to be stubborn, possibly put your life at risk just to see this through. Though I expect every. Single. Detail. I'll be okay, I promise."

He seemed satisfied with that.

"You shouldn't be too bored," he repeated. "Most importantly, if I can find you some acceptable pencils, I know you can amuse yourself for hours sketching people with or without their knowledge. I've seen you do it at restaurants, coffee shops and even on the tube over the years. Now I think of it, I bet if you suggested the sketches could be presents for their families a few of the guys would enjoy it."

"That sounds like fun," she agreed with a warm smile, pleased and touched he thought so much about her comfort and enjoyment. "While I'm at it, I can dig up all the secret gossip on you. Old tales and sordid innuendo. I'm sure I can find a way to pass a bit of time, don't worry."

"If I wasn't such a strong man, Sal, I'd be worried."

He kissed her, but she could tell he was teasing her. Nothing worried her Bobby, he was the strongest, most wonderful man in the universe.

"El and I shouldn't be too long," he added. "I promise we'll be brief as we can manage."

"Find me that sketch book and make certain you point out where those lockers and camp beds you've told me about before are, so I can nap if I get too worn out, and I'll wait until you're ready," she said.

"I love you," he murmured.

The strength in his tone proved to her how deeply he meant those words.

"I know," she replied back impishly.

He blinked at her in surprise for a moment, and she drew the seconds of silence out. She laughed, then kissed him hard. She hugged him tightly.

"I love you more than anything in the whole world," she whispered in his ear, like it was some desperate secret. "Even more than paints. Or that perfect ray of morning sunlight. More than anything."

He chuckled, and she was pleased to see the edge of worry and tension had seeped out of him. She knew he had to work, knew it would all come crashing back on him soon, but for now, he was light and carefree, and she loved having a hand to help with that.

"Notebooks and pencils," he murmured.

They kissed again, then he seemed to tear himself away. Sally watched, cherishing every moment as he hunted through his desk, looking for the small items that would distract her until he returned from his mission.

* * * *

"El," Rob called out. He led Sally into the office.

His partner looked up, her red hair pulled back into a pony tail. She's been bent over, saying something to

James and raised her hand when she saw him, indicating Rob to come closer.

"Sal—" Rob began, but Sally cut him off.

"No, Bobby, it might be the painting. Maybe they've found something new. I'm a part of this, I deserve to know. "

Forced to concede that point, Rob sighed. They both made their way to where El and James hovered over her desk. A large sheet of paper had blurred black and white smudges everywhere. Rob frowned, not recognizing it as...well, anything. He glanced at El, waiting for an explanation.

"It's the view of the night sky, albeit blown up. Ben gave the digital images to Julia and while I think her curiosity was aroused, she's also in the devil of a mood."

"Do we risk going to see her?" Rob didn't feel foolish asking.

Julia was far and away one of their best analysts— anything and everything to do with topographical searches were her forte. But she was not a woman to be rushed, bullied or coerced. Her temper was legendary around the Agency and only her undisputed skill kept everyone accepting the more demanding side of her personality.

"Promise her chocolates, a large box of the good stuff," El suggested. "Because, yes, I think we should at least talk to her before we go interview Chambers. We need every scrap of information we can get."

Rob held only a little trepidation as they walked down a maze of corridors through the labyrinth of offices until they came to a plain, unmarked wooden door. Rob knew Julia preferred to keep this miniscule office because, to the unknowing agent, the room could easily be mistaken for a cleaner's closet.

Julia had told him a number of times it kept the riff raff away.

Privately, he thought she simply liked the privacy, but it amounted to the same thing, anyway.

Rob cast a final glance to El.

She shook her head in the negative.

"You knock, mate. You're the one with the sweet smile and promise of chocolates," she insisted.

Rob sighed then knocked. Determined to convey the importance of the situation, he opened the door before Julia could refuse them admittance.

"Your choice of dark almond slivered truffles, or the heart-shaped romance bulk box of chocolate, Jules," he said as he stuck his head in the doorway.

Julia lifted her face to stare at him. When she tilted her head to the side, he knew she'd be able to see he had other people with him. She blinked behind her glasses.

"For four of you in this tiny office they keep me in?" she replied crankily, "we can start with the truffles and negotiate for whatever else you're here to hassle me over. I'm assuming you and El are on the Cezanne case?"

Considering there were no expletives and she hadn't threatened to throw him from the room, Rob took it as tantamount to a welcome. They all crammed into the tiny office. He peered at her screen and saw she'd divided it into four quadrants. He recognized some of it, but not all and figured Julia would enjoy explaining it to them.

"Tell me a story." He tilted his chin to indicate her work.

"This is worse than looking for a needle in a haystack," she complained, though she sounded more challenged than bitter or resentful. "I've ended up writing a code to calculate all the angles. I've guessed the average height of person — I'm working on five nine since we don't even know whether its male or female. I'm starting at what I hope will be a logical place, between the man and woman embracing in the picture. That seems to be the focal point for the painting."

"Those sound like fair assumptions," El said.

Julia cast her a glance and nodded her appreciation.

"That was the easy part. I'm not a code freak, but it wasn't too taxing to write it up and apply it here. Plus it will save me time having to run another analysis to get the computer to manually keep tabs of each of the constellations and degrees and...you probably don't really care about all that, I can already see your eyes glazing. Okay, so with that taken care of, now I need to run simultaneous searches from a bunch of different data bases worldwide. This is where it gets tricky, because most of them run on varying systems. Some are considered sensitive documents, which means security to bypass and try to manipulate. Add onto that our favorite issue of running multiple scans on a global scale through a series of permutations because we don't know exactly what we're looking for. I'm running blind here in too many ways. I don't know how the data we have fits into anything. And of course we want answers quickly..."

Julia looked around at them. Rob could follow in theory, but he knew he was out of his depth and didn't understand the full ramifications of what she was trying to express. He glanced at El, who seemed determined to not show she was mystified, though even he could see the flicker in her eye to show she wasn't following. Sally appeared genuinely interested but baffled and James was impossible to read — which Rob took to mean he wasn't on top of it either.

Seeming to grasp this, Julia sighed. Rob could all but see her rearrange the data she longed to share and simplify it.

"We need to keep the parameters wide so we don't miss anything," she said.

They all agreed.

"And we're not just working with one or two variables, but lots of them. We don't know the starting point from the painting to the sky. So we're very unsure of many of the angles. Without that, it's stabbing in the dark — almost literally — to try and relate that into a specific place in reality."

"Okay, that I can follow," Rob agreed. "So how are you going to do it?"

Julia threw him a sour look.

"I'm holding firm to a few assumptions. Firstly we only have data that goes back a certain amount of time. I can't work with something I don't have, so I'm going to get the best fit for the decades of information we do have. If this painting precedes that, then we're screwed. Second, I'm assuming it's a visual representation and not something tricky, like through a telescope or field glasses. Other than that, I'm hoping to just get lucky."

"So it's just a matter of time for the computer to chew through all the possible places?" El asked, her voice ringing with hopefulness.

Julia's computer chimed and she continued to speak as she clicked her mouse over a bunch of her windows.

"I'm hoping I can narrow it to a single system fairly soon. I'm taking up a lot of the computer's capabilities by doing dozens of searches on different areas. Think of it like…my computer is trying to speak Japanese to Japan, Korean to Korea, Swahili, Arabic, Russian, German and so on. And it's not just the language itself—it's the operating systems, the sensitivity, politics and all sorts of layers you don't even want to know about."

"Rob and I are about to go and interview Erik Chambers, the man who organized the touch up, presumably after this information was added," El said. "Is there anything else you can give us, something we should be on the lookout for?"

Julia mumbled for a moment, her focus riveted on the screen. Rob watched as she flicked through a seemingly endless group of tabs one after the other. He waited. She was clearly caught up in something.

"Son of a bitch," Julia turned to grin in triumph at first El then at him. "I'll deny this later if it's proven wrong, but my best guess at this moment is we're looking at a Tibet, China, Mongolia type of range. I'm going to leave Russia in there just in case, they're all quite incestuous—when it comes to technology, secrets and politics, I mean. The lines are very blurred and there's tons of crossovers and I don't want to narrow our range too early on. But I'll bet you a second box of those delicious truffles we'll end up proving it's somewhere around there."

Rob squeezed her shoulder in thanks. "You're a gem and worth every penny for those chocolates. Text me if you find anything else we can work on and I'll throw in a bottle of Champagne."

Hopeful for the first time since they'd been called in on this case, Rob left Julia's office finally feeling like they were getting a handle on things.

Chapter Six

"Do you think James will be okay back at HQ?" Rob asked.

El was driving and seemed determined to skirt as close to the posted speed limits as possible. His question was not idle, but based in the curiosity of whether she was speeding because she wanted to get home and sleep—something he couldn't blame her for—or because she didn't trust James to behave himself alone back at their office.

"I'm half tempted to joke and say he'll have corrupted half the night shift by the time we return, but I'm afraid it'll be a little too close to the truth."

Even though she spoke like it was a dark confession, Rob wasn't fooled. He could see the happy glow in his partner's eyes. He liked seeing her happy, he'd been disappointed for her when circumstances had come between them these last few months.

"If he teaches Sally how to pick a lock, I'll have to kill him," he teased. "Now if we talk about some of the younger agents who have been hired recently, I wouldn't mind at all if James taught them a few of his skills. Those young guys could do with a few good scares. I can just imagine Waldron, or Preston, or a number of the other team leaders chewing them out for skirting too close to the line or getting caught with a bit of breaking and entering. Will do them good to have their egos deflated a little."

"Oh, please, like we never toed the line."

"Back in my day..." Rob said in a craggy voice, mimicking an old timer starting off on his war story. As he'd hoped, he made El laugh.

"Okay." She gasped to catch her breath again.

He noticed she'd lessened the pressure on the accelerator too. "That made me feel good. So tell me again about Chambers."

"Sally said when Vicky was dying, she identified him as the man who hired to her touch up the painting," Rob said. He forced himself to not relive those scary minutes, remembered that Sal was fine, and safe, and probably charming everyone in her vicinity right about now.

"And this bloke is a recluse," El continued with a frown. "Does that really mean he can't be the one behind all this? I hate to sound like a wimp, but do you think we should arrive with back up?"

Rob patted his pocket, comforted by the weight of his .25 against his thigh.

"This was as handy as a brick around my neck at Vicky's," he pointed out. "But I'm not completely ignorant. I've been thinking about the different approaches to all these attacks too, and it doesn't make sense them coming from the same source. Take the initial heist, the one Chelsea and David worked undercover on. That was professional. They were a proper team full of experience and knowledge. And they were successful in stealing the painting. Then there was the bomb on the safe you and James cracked, again, professional, but more rudimentary than the smuggling ring. And lastly we have these wannabe gangsters driving by and shooting the hell out of a house to kill one of the links connecting everything together."

"Put like that, there's definitely a decreasing level of skill at work here," El agreed. "When you compare the initial attack on the Gallery to the method of taking out Vicky Parker, there's a world of difference."

"Which leads me back to thinking maybe there's more than one group of people in play here."

"Wasn't there going to be a silent auction of the painting?" El frowned.

"That would mean more than one party would definitely have knowledge about the painting. But that doesn't immediately mean they know about the code."

El slanted him a mild glare.

"Rob, if you were trying to sell something, particularly if you wanted to milk every penny and raise the price as high as possible, wouldn't *you* send rumors flying around? The more people talking about the piece, the more the gossips hear and the more interest you pique. That related directly to the price people are willing to pay."

"True," Rob conceded with a nod. "Okay, that fits. None of it helps us yet, but it fits together."

"I think if we can find out what this damn code is and neutralize it, we can put this baby to bed." El indicated and turned into the driveway of the estate.

Almost immediately, enormous, ornate gates blocked their path. An intercom was lit by a modern-looking digital display panel. A light shined over it, glowing brightly in the darkness of the early evening.

Rob noticed at least half a dozen monitors and cameras facing in every direction.

This was a man who took his privacy and security very seriously.

El wound down her window. She reached out and pressed the button. Static sounded, then a dignified voice spoke.

"Chambers' residence, you're speaking with Mr Burnt."

El cast him an incredulous look, clearly torn somewhere between laughter and amazement. Rob leaned closer and spoke loudly, projecting his voice out of the window.

"Good evening, Mr Burnt," he replied, putting on his most pompous Eton accent. "Mr Stevens and Ms Williams here to speak with Mr Chambers, please. We're with an Agency that is working in conjunction with the Department of Special Research. We're here to inquire about the London Gallery and a particular painting."

"Nice," El mouthed to him.

Rob shrugged. He'd hopefully given Chambers' man enough information to whet his master's interest but not enough to scare him away. There was a pause where Rob presumed Mr Burnt relayed the information to Chambers. Almost a minute later there was an audible click and the wrought iron gates began to slowly swing open.

"Please park near the trees at the end of the drive," Mr Burnt said. "You will be met."

There was static for a second then silence. El and Rob waited for the gates to finish swinging open.

"I'm glad one of us is articulate," she mumbled.

"I spent a fair bit of time with my grandparents," Rob explained. "Good articulation and enunciation was often the difference between a second piece of shortbread with my tea or having to wait for dinner."

El chuckled and put the car into gear as the gates rumbled to a stop.

"You are full of surprises, aren't you?"

Rob grinned but didn't feel anything further needed to be said.

At the end of the drive was a large circle where cars could turn around. Trees shaded the area and, as instructed, El parked there. French doors on the side of the house were open and a butler stood waiting for them. The house reeked of money but managed to not be ostentatious.

Rob climbed from the car. He walked around the bonnet to meet El. He fell into step beside her and they walked in tandem toward the butler, presenting a united front. Despite the age of the man, his wrinkled face and thinning hair, his back was ramrod straight, his posture perfect. He tilted his head courteously and greeted them with all the dignity his voice had promised over the intercom.

"Mr Stevens. Ms Williams. Mr Chambers is in the sitting room awaiting you. I feel it pertinent to add he is not in perfect health and usually retires early. You indicated a wish to ask some questions, I hope it won't take long?"

"Hopefully not very," Rob replied. He kept his tone somewhat formal but firm. Neither he nor El would be bullied or manipulated, but they could be perfectly polite about their investigation unless Chambers or anyone else gave them cause to be rougher.

Chambers' man seemed appeased by this. He led them inside, through what looked to be a library, down a long corridor and into a smaller, more warmly heated room. The house was stately, with enormous ceilings, plenty of dark mahogany paneling and the feel of age. Rob would have bet a week's wage it was a family home. The paintings gracing the walls, the sculpture and art, just the overall sense was of a home that had seen much love and usage, and would only temporarily be quiet as it was now.

Mr Burnt opened the door, announced them then stepped back to grant them admittance. Rob almost felt as if he had fallen fifty or a hundred years back into the past. This was reiterated as he entered the den.

A large but still cozy area had a fire crackling merrily along one wall. An enormous desk took up a good portion of the back, with floor-to-ceiling windows looking out across the back lawn. Some hunting and landscape paintings filled the walls and except for the very modern computer, telephone and office set-up, he doubted the room had changed much over the course of a generation or two. Rob followed El inside. Both of them made a beeline for the fireplace where there were three wing-back chairs forming a semi-circle around the grate. Mr Burnt entered last, closing the door behind them. Mr Burnt walked to a side table where a silver tray held two brandy decanters and another tray of crystal cut glasses.

Only as Rob got closer did he see the elderly man in one of the chairs, a woolen rug wrapped around his legs. His arms were spindly, his face even more weathered than Burnt's. He sat comfortably back in the chair, but it was only in the faint wheeze of his breath that it was clear this man was not particularly hearty.

"You'll excuse me if I don't stand," he said with slow, careful precision and a low tone. "Please, make yourselves comfortable. Would either of you care for a drink? I have some excellent scotch, or a snifter of brandy, if the lady prefers?"

El declined and took a seat. Rob paused for just a moment to take a quick gauge of Chambers before moving to the final chair and sitting.

"None for me, thank you, I'm still on the job," he explained.

Chambers nodded, lifted a hand and accepted the balloon glass Burnt handed him with a few inches of what Rob guessed would be the scotch in it.

Chambers held the glass in almost steady hands. Despite his evident frailty, his mind appeared sharp, his words didn't slur and the dark brown eyes were clear. Rob guessed this man would have been a force to be reckoned with ten years ago. He decided their questioning wouldn't harm Chambers, and indeed might even give the man a bit of a spark to his week.

Rob was glad he hadn't come up against him in the height of his power. This was a canny, strong-willed man. Rob didn't think he was a criminal, though, and that had his posture relaxing and some of his guard lowering. Sitting forward on his chair, Rob clasped his hands around his knee to convey subconsciously they were just having an easy, friendly conversation.

"Please understand while my partner and I will need to make note of this conversation, only the details pertinent to our investigation will be expounded upon," Rob started. "Our aim here is not to pry into your charity work, nor sully your reputation. But it has come to our attention that a particular piece of artwork—a Cezanne—has been encoded. We believe this occurred in recent years and it's caused quite a stir and resulted in a number of deaths. Have you been following the news?"

"I heard about the Gallery being attacked, if that's what you're inferring, yes. I didn't know anything had occurred to that painting though, no," Chambers replied bluntly. His tone showed no aggression and only mild curiosity.

"Were you aware the painting had a series of numbers and letters painted into it? We've been reliably informed that you purchased it, arranged to have it restored over those specific areas and then donated it to the Gallery," El said with equal force but no heat.

"Of course I know that junk was written into it, that's why I had Miss Parker paint over it. Thought she did a damn fine job of it too. Certainly did the trick. Almost five years that painting has been in the Gallery's possession and only this week has there been any trouble over it. Tell me, how did you find the code?"

"Some of our experts discovered it during a routine analysis after we received it," Rob replied, following quickly with another of his questions. "Do you know the decryption key for the code? Or what the text actually is?" He had the feeling Chambers knew well the dance of interrogation—how to answer a question by parrying it with another. The give and take was well known.

"That I don't," Chambers replied with evident regret. "I bought the piece quietly from a man in China who wanted to finance his defection. It wasn't quite a black market purchase but neither was it strictly legitimate either. I spent a lovely few years enjoying the piece privately. When I felt it would be better suited for many people to appreciate, I did a very thorough analysis. I was still my own expert back in those days. I wanted to be absolutely positive it was a Cezanne, and legitimate before I risked my reputation in selling it."

At the mention of China, Rob glanced at El in what he hoped would be a casual gesture. She met his eyes silently and he knew she'd caught the potential significance of that tidbit too.

"Why didn't you examine it when you bought it?" El asked when Chambers paused in his reminiscence.

Chambers' eyes rose and he nodded respectfully at El, seeming pleased by her insight.

"I was pretty certain it was legitimate," he said after a moment's sip of the scotch. "More than enough to enjoy the piece in the privacy of my own home. My reputation, however, is one of the few things I have left and when I'm gone it will be the only lasting impression I can leave. I have no children, no family, so my works, deeds and reputation are all I have. I needed to be absolutely positive the piece was genuine before I sold it as such."

El murmured her thanks, seeming satisfied.

Chambers picked up the thread and continued again. "I had Burnt make a few discreet enquiries when I discovered the code. Without finer details, he managed to find a friend of a friend who was good with decryption. It took him a few days, and he was very excited initially. To a casual observation, the data is a formula to amass alternative energy. The impressionable lad tapped a friend of *his* and started looking into it before he got back to me. I could have told him it was bunk, but the damage was done."

"And so the stories started to circulate," Rob added in a soft tone.

Chambers shook his head. "Not quite. I'm not one for idle gossip and as I'd gone to great pains to make certain Burnt gave no particulars of where the code was sourced from, there was no connection to be made."

Rob frowned, trying to understand how the Cezanne could have been linked with the code if this was the case.

"Word has reached me that a code could be found in the painting," Chambers offered. "I'm uncertain whether anyone has actually managed to decode it as I have, but until this week, I was not worried. As the writings can be proven false, they are useless."

"But no one knows this except for yourself," El pointed out dryly. "Human nature being what it is, once the painting was identified, everyone wanted to have it and this secret. People died, are still dying over it. Why didn't you come forward with this when you discovered it?"

"What is life without some mystery? If everything is known there can be no wonder, no magic. Please" — he held up a hand as El opened her mouth to speak — "I understand what you're saying, and I agree. But you're talking with the virtue of hindsight. Had I been told, or somehow psychically known my keeping quiet would result in unfortunate murders, I would, of course, have sent out word. Though honestly, without proof and visibility, who would have believed? Men fight over treasures and secrets such as these. Look at all the deaths over the alchemy of changing lead into gold. Anyone can understand it's blatantly false, but that doesn't stop people believing and hoping, does it? Treasure and mysteries have been like this for aeons."

Rob noticed El had her lips pressed together tightly. Clearly she was still unhappy, but like him, she appeared to see Chambers was speaking the truth.

"The area where the stars were drawn from—where is it?" Rob asked, hoping to give El time to settle her temper a bit.

"A small province in the mountainous region of China," Chambers replied. "Understand, I don't have the...uh...intricate level of access you have, so you might be able to find more data. But it seems to be just a small, almost empty region. A few townships, no large or intimidating structures at all."

Baffled, but not wanting to show his hand, Rob nodded as if this was what he had expected. He made a mental note to make sure they followed up on that, double-checked Chambers' findings. He believed the man, but that was no reason not to make sure there were no nasty surprises hidden, either underground or within this seemingly empty area of land.

"Is it possible for you or Mr Burnt to give us the details of the man who knows the decryption key? We have our own analysts working on it, but the faster we can unlock this text, hopefully the quicker we can stop the violence occurring." Rob stood, sensing Erik had given them everything he could.

"Of course," the elder man replied. He reached out to take the small bell on the spindly legged table near his chair. Ringing it, he summoned Mr Burnt. After only a few moments, the doors opened.

"Yes, sir?"

"Leonard, please give Ms Williams and Mr Stevens the contact details of that enterprising young man who decoded the Cezanne's secrets. Oh, will that be all?"

El had stood while Chambers spoke. Rob caught her gaze. She nodded to indicate she was willing to leave. Glancing back at Chambers, Rob tilted his head in a nod.

"Yes, you've been most helpful, thank you, Mr Chambers."

"My pleasure. Please excuse me for not seeing you out, but Burnt can take care of you."

They exchanged their farewells and Rob stepped to the side to let El go first. Something about the house, or maybe the courtly, semi-formal tone to the whole interview had his latent chivalrous self coming to the fore. Burnt closed the door behind them and held out a card to El, who stood closer to him.

"I've been following the news, and from what you said earlier managed to piece together the basics," Burnt said. "Shannon Hansen was the man who did the work for me, and that's the number I contacted him on, though it's many years ago now. If you feel I can be of more service, my own contact details are below Mr Hansen's."

El nodded.

Satisfied, Rob held his hand out to shake Burnt's. He and El were silent as they walked back to the car. Rob ran over everything in his mind, analyzing it for things he might have missed, tones, inflections and anything else that could help them wrap this up quickly.

Chapter Seven

A few minutes down the road, after having chewed on his thoughts for a while, Rob pulled out his phone and quickly texted Julia.

Chambers said origin of C was China. I owe you a second box. Rob.

"I believe him," he said. "I've texted Julia that Erik said the painting originated in China."

El nodded. "Unfortunately, I believe him too, though I bet Julia will continue with her search exactly as she'd planned. She's not one for cutting corners or speeding her work up because we want data faster. Dammit, it would have been much simpler if Chambers had an agenda, or something we could push to finish this. The truth is always better than neat and tidy. It just rarely makes our work easier."

"Agreed," Rob said.

They were both quiet, each lost in their own thoughts.

Rob enjoyed puzzling through their various options. His brain was an analytical one for the most part. He enjoyed the comfortable peace between his partner and himself and ran though scenarios, trying to find a good fit that satisfied his innate sense of justice while also resulting in the safety of Sally and others who came into contact with the painting.

"Once Masters has decoded the text, I think there's a way to wrap this all up," he finally said. "It might mean twisting the Gallery's arm, though."

"After all the death, violence and destruction this has caused, I'm sure we can pitch it to Waldron in a palatable way he can enforce up the chain," El said wryly. "Run it by me, just so we can be on the same page."

Rob nodded, glad that El was willing to support him without even hearing his plan. Not that he'd made one yet. They always worked best as a team, so he started thinking aloud to see what she thought of his ideas.

"We'll need to refine the pitch before we make it to Waldron, but here's the gist of it. Let's assume Masters can crack this thing and have a transcription of the text in the next twenty-four to thirty-six hours. The guy's good and tenacious and hates to be beaten, so it's a decent bet to make."

"I'd almost say a pessimistic one," El agreed, concentrating fully on the road as they zoomed back to London. "Masters is one of our best. He might have it done as early as tomorrow morning, especially if he has one of those epiphanies he's known for."

Rob agreed with her assessment.

"Okay, so we assume he has our answers in a short enough timeframe that we can act on them before we have to release physical custody of the painting." Rob paused.

El nodded that she was with him so far.

"The problem all along with this has been secrets," Rob continued. "Various factions have only had part of the story—either they know there's a code or they know somewhere in the painting is important information or even they've heard a mangled telling and have simply taken away the painting is important, special. Whatever. They're all fighting amongst themselves to get the prize. So we go public in a big way. We splash the 'secret information' all over the news, the papers, the Internet and leak the works. I know it's not our usual course of mingling the truth with a pretty fictional story, or even just burying the lot of it and spinning the media, but this is beyond that."

He knew what he was suggesting was risky, but he honestly thought going public would be the safest route in the long term. He watched El as she drove, interested to know how she felt about it. Often it was he who came up with the crazy ideas and she who refined them into working solutions.

El frowned, seeming to think over his proposal.

"Enough groups know pieces of the truth and a whitewash or clever story isn't going to jibe with what they have," El said.

"Exactly," Rob agreed readily. "We can't release twelve stories pandering to the different bits and nuggets they all have—hell, my gut says we don't even know all the parties currently invested in this. It's all moot anyway. We can only go with one version of the story, which leans me toward insisting on the truth."

"That means we need to be a hundred percent certain the data—whatever it turns out to be—is safe for public consumption. That's a big ask when we haven't even got the proper script yet." El shook her head.

"I know. That bit might need finessing," Rob admitted, willing to agree to the holes in his plan. "But even if it is dangerous—or let's go with sensitive for now—surely making it public property and on every Internet search engine would lessen the sting."

"Having 'how to make a bomb in ten easy steps' pages on the Internet hasn't stopped people blowing each other up," El pointed out.

"But neither do you hear endlessly of bombs going off day in and day out. If people want that information badly enough, they're going to do it, regardless of how much effort they need to expend."

There was a short silence as they both thought. Rob tried to find a serious problem with his solution, but it seemed the best way to get this all out into the open. He waited to hear what El thought.

"What about the stars in the sky?" El questioned, seeming to be thinking now along a different track. "I'm wondering if it's a reference to maybe a laboratory, or where they ran experiments. Something sinister. What do you make of it?"

"I'm sure with satellite maps and all the topography references we have, Jules and the lab can look into it easily. But...you know what?" Rob replied thoughtfully. "I'd like to think it's just a view of the sky, a reference to where the man who added these details was, lived or maybe worked. Nothing more than that. What if the guy who added that text added the stars as a kind of graffiti, like kids who carve 'I woz ere' or the date into a tree. I mean, there's no data in the stars, it's just a reference point, a very geeky way of signaling where you were. I'm inclined to believe it's just his idea of a signature, or a joke," Rob suggested.

El chuckled. "I can actually see that too, although I'll feel better when we have a location for it. Bet you anything once we release that detail it will become a kind of Mecca, with pilgrims and a load of tourists taking photos."

Rob nodded, inclined to agree. They drove in silence.

"Well, I'm with you on all of this in theory, partner," El said. "I'm just not sure we can convince Waldron — let alone the Gallery — to get on board if the text is going to pose a threat."

"The Gallery I've already accounted for," Rob replied, feeling proud of himself. "We sell it to them as a special feature. It's not a stretch. The Cezanne gets bills and publicized around the globe as the painting of secrets, or some such catchy name, and they sell UV glasses, or have tours every half hour where they shine UV light over the painting and people can see the code for themselves. Then around the painting itself you'd have panels up like a museum, a visible transcript of what the code says, plus the key and a translation. If it is a science-type fuel cell thing you'd have other panels explaining it in laymen's terms."

"Damn," El said, seeming to be struck by his plan. "They'll lap that up with a fucking spoon. I can totally see it. The Gallery will get a kick, charge an extra admittance fee for that specific showing. They'll add in audio guides, special tour groups — at even more expense — and wristbands for VIP screenings. I take it back, you won't have any problems selling that to the Gallery or its patrons. They'll be beating down the door to see it all for themselves. The extra traffic alone will have them falling all over themselves to stake claim for the idea."

"Yeah, I thought they'd manage to turn it into a profit-making machine, probably end up cheesy as hell, too. They'll have models of the damage the Gallery sustained in the raid and dioramas of the exact route the thieves took."

"Oh, man," El snickered. "Chelsea and David will die if they become infamous. I can see it now, all the fresh-faced recruits in Dublin, pointing and whispering amongst themselves. 'Those are the two who blew up the Gallery and helped steal the famous Cezanne'. It will almost make the sleep deprivation worth it if I can hold that over their heads."

"I think you should stay, let James and Sally sit in on us reporting to Waldron and making the pitch. I agree, the force of weight he puts behind it will likely rest on Chambers' information being accurate, but as long as whatever is in there is rubbish, we should be able to put this to bed."

"Not quite," El smirked.

Rob tilted his head, wondering what he'd missed. El stared at him for a moment, moving her head to check the road as she drew the moment out.

Finally he caved. "What? I can't think of something I missed, I must be more tired than I realized."

"You've got a report to write," she said smugly. "And if you don't get it in before Masters has that transcript, Waldron will be hassling us for a debrief synopsis too."

Rob groaned, slumped in the car seat, but nodded, resigned.

"I'll make a start on it before I go," he promised. "Unless Sally's about to crash, then I'll take her home.

But I won't back out. I gave you my word and I'll keep it."

"I know, that's why I'm all but doing cartwheels over here." El grinned.

Rob chuckled, tilted back on the headrest and closed his eyes. He knew there was only fifteen or twenty minutes left until they returned to the office, but he reckoned he'd need the nap. It was looking like another long night.

* * * *

A week later

"Sal?" Rob called out as he pushed open the door to her loft. His arms were full of boxes and bags of take-out, his work stuff and a recently purchased evening newspaper.

She watched while he balanced everything and removed his keys from the lock. She'd been waiting for him to arrive, equal parts nervous and excited.

This was a massive day for her, one she'd been worried about and simultaneously looking forward to for months. Never in her wildest dreams could she have believed so much would have changed, particularly between them, but that made her more emotional now the time had finally come.

Rob looked around her studio flat and a jolt of lust seared through her as he spotted her near the far windows, pretending to paint on the single easel set up there.

"There's only about ten more minutes of good light," she mumbled, "but I've been waiting for this for too long, I'm not going to get anywhere now you're finally here."

She started to clean her brushes, surreptitiously watching Rob while he shut the door behind him and went over to the kitchenette. He placed the take-out on the tiny bench. Sally had unofficially moved into his flat, though the loft was a perfect studio and she couldn't give it up.

Thankfully, he understood that and hadn't even tried asking. Somehow life had turned blissful after the mess of their case had cleared. They'd fallen into the now-familiar routine of him meeting her here after work. Then they'd either go out for dinner or he'd bring something over and they'd end up at his place, make passionate love and fall asleep together in a tangle of limbs.

It was a way of life she could easily get used to.

Sally placed her brushes carefully away and as she came across the room, she noticed Rob looking at the paper.

"National Gallery Shows Secret Code Cezanne!" screamed the headline in enormous font.

She paused, surprised. It wasn't uncommon for the 'real world' to pass her by, particularly when she'd been as consumed by a project like the paintings she'd just finished. Still, Sally was shocked she hadn't caught wind of this. Clearly Bobby was letting her know in his own way.

"Is that story all over the place?" she asked, bemused.

"Every paper and many of the tabloids are running with it in various formats," he confirmed. "I've been tempted to purchase one of the sleazier magazines, which had run with the byline *'Secret Chinese code proven false – a secret plot to destabilize Britannia and start war with France'*! Which is just…"

Sally chuckled as he shook his head.

"Come on, admit it, Bobby," she teased. Hugging him tightly, he enjoyed the feel of his warm, strong frame next to her. "You're going to buy a copy on the sly in a day or two when no one else is paying attention. You'll hide it in a closet somewhere."

He chuckled and she knew from the faint flush of color in his cheeks she'd guessed correctly.

"I just can't help but laugh at the lurid turn of phrase. Promise you won't tell my secret?"

Even though she knew he was kidding, she replied with sincere honesty.

"I won't breathe a word to a soul, Bobby."

He pressed the pad of his thumb to her lips, and for a moment they lost themselves in the special bubble that was just the two of them. She saw the moment he refocused his eyes and he came back to the point at hand.

"They've got the basics of the details correct. The views and commentary vary slightly, but the core message seems to be getting through. And as we'd hoped, the Gallery jumped on the opportunity when it was presented as a new propaganda tool. Plans are already underway with select details being 'leaked' to keep interest flared and keenly alive."

"I might start a scrap book," Sally said, quite serious.

"What? Of this stuff?"

"Of course, why not?"

Rob grimaced. "Most cases don't end up anything like this. On the rare occasion it makes the papers, it's practically unrecognizable as the truth we've uncovered. It's not always their fault, we're often responsible for misleading them, but this is an almost unique circumstance."

"I'm still going to get every paper and keep them," she insisted, stubborn in her own way.

Rob turned, wrapped his arms around her and kissed her thoroughly.

"Maybe that's a good idea. There have been many differences in this case, but I'll always remember it as the one we came to finally be together. I love you so much, Sal."

Sally grinned, knowing this love between them might falter or hit a rough patch, but nothing could shake them. She knew it with a certainty like she knew the sun would rise the following morning.

He kissed her again, and she hungrily explored his mouth. It was minutes later she realized she'd become distracted. With a moan she pulled away, breathing hard. She decided to share her surprise after they'd eaten. Something about their conversation made her want to wait just a little longer before she revealed her news. She knew she had to share before her big reception at the gallery the following week, but it didn't feel right changing the subject from something so serious onto herself.

"That food smells delicious. I worked through lunch and am starving. Let me just quickly wash the paint off my hands."

Rob nipped at her full lower lip then released her.

Sally moved to the far side of the room and started to wash her hands. It was only when she looked up as she turned off the tap that she noticed Bobby had become curious and wandered over to the piece she'd been putting the finishing touches on.

It was the surprise she'd been working on for him.

Nerves fluttered in her stomach.

She'd been adamant this last painting be included. Bobby had been caught up in meetings, debriefings and the seemingly never-ending cycle of reports, so she'd not had what felt like the right time and place to show him this final, very special, piece.

She smiled and the final thought clicked into place. Of course. She couldn't take it to him—he needed to go to it.

The painting was almost done. Bold, bright colors splashed over the canvas making it pop, to her eye. The sky was a warm blue, the sun low on the horizon. It was still light, but clearly dusk was not far away. The sky bled out to a darker navy the farther from the setting sun it went.

Front and center was a tall, dark-haired man and a shorter brunette walking arm in arm. The figures resembled herself and Bobby, but the lines were very slightly blurred, letting the viewer interpret it for themselves. She watched as Bobby peered closer. She grinned.

He'd evidently noticed the picture was like two meshed over each other. The man wore a dark suit like Bobby so often did, but there was a hint of armor, of a breastplate maybe, just hidden beneath the surface.

The painting was a blending of fantasy and reality— a specialty of hers, like the children playing with pixies and fairies—there but not quite at the same time. The woman wore a flowing summer dress, but it had an old-fashioned, almost princess style cut to it. Her face was turned to the man, her gaze blissfully happy. She hoped some of the female viewers would notice the faintest twinkle of a tiara in the woman's hair.

The couple were walking in the park, hand in hand, and the closer the viewer studied the portrait, the more she hoped they would see. That was her intention, at least. There was a dragon hidden amongst the trees, and she'd made the outline of a ring of fairies dancing on the edge of a shallow pond.

A lot of the smaller items she'd purposely left hazy, so everyone might see something slightly different.

An imp peeked out over a large rock and there was the faintest outline of a sword in the growing shadows at the man's hip and outstretched arm.

The city was in the background, where the man and woman headed toward the horizon, but some of the buildings had almost fortress-like qualities and turrets near the towers. It was a magical piece, and Sally held this painting very dear to her heart.

She hoped Rob would see how much of her heart and soul was in it.

"Do you think it's very obnoxious of me to cast myself as the princess?" she asked when she couldn't take the silence anymore. She hated to interrupt, but she was dead curious and more than a trifle nervous for his reaction.

"I love it, don't you dare sell this piece. I'll buy it for the flat. Like you, it will be perfect in there. And no, it's not obnoxious. You're my princess, my heroine, my everything. I think you deserve diamonds and jewels of all kinds."

"I'll be happy with just having my prince and my happily ever after," she murmured and went into his arms. She loved how perfectly they fitted together.

He bent and scooped her into his arms.

Sal laughed and clung tighter to him.

"Bobby, wait, what about dinner?"

"I'm famished," he insisted. "We can take the food back to my place and reheat it there. Right now I'm going to ravish my princess and be the conquering hero you continue to portray me as."

"Well now," she murmured then kissed his neck. "A girl can't argue with that then, can she?"

She let him carry her up the winding stairs, though the thin metal wasn't really made for two people at a time. Rob set her feet to the floor of the small loft area and Sally immediately went to work. She reached out and pushed his expensive jacket from his shoulders. Rob bent to remove his shoes, then his socks.

As was becoming the norm for them, what started as a sweet, slow revealing of their flesh was soon hasty and desperate. In seconds they were both naked. Sally grabbed Rob's hands and pulled him with her onto the bed.

"Oh, no you don't," he chuckled. "This time I want to be in charge. You make me lose my mind, Sal. I want to indulge in some fantasies this time."

She raised an eyebrow, curious and feeling cocky that she apparently wielded such power over him.

"Okay," she said slowly, "what did you have in mind?"

"Nothing too sinister," he reassured her. "Or not this time. I just seem to always find myself rushing after you, not enjoying the thrill of having you here."

She shivered when he palmed her naked breasts, using his fingers to toy with her hard nipples. Suddenly, doing things Rob's way didn't sound like something she should fight.

"Go for it, Bobby," she purred. "What would you like?"

Without answering, he lowered his hands from her breasts to her hips, manipulating her body so she rested on hands and knees upon the bed. She could feel the heat radiating from his skin as he followed her onto the sheets. The thin, wiry hair on his thighs scratched her ever so faintly and heightened her awareness of his large frame lurking behind her.

He probed her labia lips with one finger, and caressed his thumb over her clit. Gasping, her body reacted like she'd been struck by lightning. Her nipples hardened further, her skin got goosebumps and her pussy grew damp. He stroked over her plump flesh with his fingers, the digits caressing her.

She glanced behind her, and the look of ecstasy on his face was enough to have her heart pounding. He drank her in with those dark eyes. She loved the flush over his skin, proving he wanted her as much as she him. When she moved one hand back to touch him, he shook his head.

"Not this time, Sal." His voice was deeper than usual, lust thickening it. "It's my turn."

She grinned wickedly. "That means next time is mine," she warned him.

He nodded.

Satisfied, she turned back, her heart jolting as he thrust three fingers deeply inside her. When he stroked her arsehole with his other hand, her legs wobbled and the breath rushed out of her lungs.

"Grab the headboard, Sal," Rob ordered.

After only the faintest of pauses she did so. He pumped his fingers inside her, caressed her inner walls for obeying.

The world exploded in color behind her closed eyelids. Breathing became difficult, but who needed air when her body sang under his ministrations? The world narrowed to the perfect bubble encasing them.

Noting else mattered.

For years she'd known Rob to be a man of total control, able to compartmentalize himself and stay strong when he needed to do the work he did. But she'd never imagined him to be such a determined lover. He played her body to perfection.

Sweating, she pleaded with him. "Now, Rob. My clit, stroke it harder. I need to come."

"Not yet," he said.

She gnashed her teeth, caught somewhere between bliss and pain from being deprived of the orgasm she could sense just out of reach.

She wanted to feel his thick cock, wanted that inner stretch she loved when he penetrated her fully. She wanted his fingers pinching her nipples and to lose all sense of reality as he took her to heights she'd never believed possible.

Sally unclenched one hand from the headboard, but she hadn't even managed to move it before his voice rang out sharply.

"Put that back, Sal. My turn, remember?"

"Then fucking do it," she panted, almost crazy for completion.

He continued to toy with her, though. He'd thrust the fingers inside her, but then stop before she could angle herself to force him to tease her G-spot. He'd tweak her nipples, or rub his thumb over her puckered back hole with his other hand, but then move on before she could push herself over.

She needed to come. Urgently. The desire he'd worked up in her was like a ball cramping inside her chest and stomach.

Release was only a few breaths away.

Then finally, *finally* he withdrew the fingers inside her. She sobbed in relief. Rob shifted on the bed, reached out to grab a foil packet, and she couldn't help herself. Sally pressed on his shoulder and pushed him onto his side. She took the condom from his hand then broke it open.

With a grin that made her heart melt, Rob let her have her way. He lay down on his back, his erection stiff and proud, jutting out from his body. She sheathed then straddled him.

"Don't think you're getting off that easy," he murmured.

Too far gone to care what he meant, Sally lifted herself off then guided him into her pussy. She exhaled loudly as they came together, his thick, hard length pressing deeply into her body and satisfying her the way she'd craved for years.

When she canted her hips up, she didn't think anything of the fact he moved a hand down around her bottom. It was only when she felt him spread her arse cheeks with his fingers that his earlier comment suddenly meant something.

Each time she sank on him, he caressed the tip of his finger over and around her tiny hole. Teasing her while she rode him hard.

"I don't think—" she started, but rational thought left her as he found some nerves just on the edge of her entrance. Shuddering, she struggled for breath. "I've not done that before, Bobby."

"And we won't this time," he replied. "I don't have the patience right now to prepare you properly. Think of it as a hint of what will come when I take my turn."

Heat washed over her, a confusing mix of emotions she didn't have the energy to sort through—embarrassment, eagerness, pleasure and a small well of desire. Things would never be boring with Bobby, that was a certainty.

She leaned over him, pressed her breasts into his muscled chest. In doing so, she knew that she exposed her arse better for him. He teased around her small hole. Rob thrust his hips up as she moved her pelvis.

Together they fucked each other, and Sally couldn't breathe so hard did her heart pound.

She loved this man more than anything. Life was perfect.

In seconds they were both coming, yelling loudly with their climaxes. Sally felt colors in every shade wash over her, the perfection of the moment only heightened with Rob's naughty finger prying into her arse. He didn't get far — his finger so big and her hole so small — but the nerves sang with pleasure and pain, a blend that sent her pulse skyrocketing. The heat of his cock pulsing inside her pussy.

They collapsed onto her bead. Sweating and panting.

When Sally caught her breath, she chuckled, feeling proud of herself.

"You hijacked my turn," Rob said.

Although his words were strong, there was no heat or threat behind them. Or none she couldn't handle.

"You were taking too long," she said. She stifled a small yawn.

"We can eat later," Rob agreed. "But I get another go."

"Not a chance, I want to be in control next time."

Rob remained silent, but his smirk said plenty. She grinned then snuggled closer to him. Another yawn escaped and she closed her eyes. Sally had no doubt there'd be many more discussions along these lines in the years to come. And that they'd be together. For always.

About the Author

Elizabeth Lapthorne has been writing professionally since 2002. She has a number of books released and is continually surprised by how much fun she has starting a new book and discovering new characters and situations that they put themselves in. She enjoys going to the gym (usually to chew over her latest problem scene), is rarely without a partially read book and has a weakness for chocolate.

Elizabeth Lapthorne loves to hear from readers. You can find her contact information, website details and author profile page at http://www.totallybound.com.

Totally Bound Publishing